Ebony Eyes

Ebony Eyes

A Murder Mystery

Maureen Stevenson

iUniverse, Inc.
New York Bloomington Shanghai

Ebony Eyes
A Murder Mystery

Copyright © 2008 by Maureen Stevenson

iUniverse books may be ordered through booksellers or by contacting:

iUniverse
1663 Liberty Drive
Bloomington, IN 47403
www.iuniverse.com
1-800-Authors (1-800-288-4677)

Because of the dynamic nature of the Internet, any Web addresses or links contained in this book may have changed since publication and may no longer be valid.

This is a work of fiction. All of the characters, names, incidents, organizations, and dialogue in this novel are either the products of the author's imagination or are used fictitiously.

ISBN: 978-0-595-50699-6 (pbk)
ISBN: 978-0-595-61616-9 (ebk)

Printed in the United States of America

CHAPTER 1

He sits in the dark. The voices, jumbled and angry, surround him but he does not hear. His eyes are closed and his mind is elsewhere in the dark recesses of his sub conscious. He hates the voices. They tell him to do things, and he hates to fight them. The time for death is soon.

*   *   *   *

Hailey gazed out her deck window into the dawn sky. Sleeping late had never been an option for as long as she could remember. She always had to be the first up, to gaze into the morning sky and breathe in the crisp air. She truly loved it. Every now and then, when she was feeling restless, she would go for a quick jog to help kick-start her mind. Not today, though; today she was finishing up some last-minute repairs on her baby.

Since she first left the Marines, she had picked up the hobby of rebuilding a 1965 Mustang GT to help ease herself back into the "real world," as her ex-shrink put it. Now, after three years, she'd finally get to take her on the road and see how well she ran. She went into her bedroom and donned some old sweats and a tee and went out to her workshop.

*   *   *   *

It was seven in the morning. Rye Jackson stretched his long frame and stood up. He'd been working since last night at eight. Everywhere he turned young bodies lay, awaiting examination. Sometimes he hated being one of the lead coroners for Seattle. Finally, he thought, I get to go home and relax for a day. Maybe I'll take Mocca for a walk along the beach, then I'll go for a swim. Perfect. He sauntered out of his office and down the hall to hand in his last report. "Hey there, Joe. How's your morning looking?"

"Not too bad, Rye. Long night?"

"Hell yes. I can't wait to go home and relax. Gonna take Mocca for a walk."

1

"She still kickin'? She's gotta be getting up there in doggie years."

"She's still got a few good ones left, Joe. Besides, she's my baby, so don't talk like that. See you tomorrow." He left Joe Brown in the supervisor's office, and jogged down the stairs to the parking level. Once Rye was on the freeway, he cranked his stereo.

*   *   *   *

Climbing. There's nothing like the rush of crawling straight up a sheer cliff face with nothing to save your life. Bobby Stein wished that that was where he was, instead of sitting behind a desk looking at the same old shit he had looked at everyday for the past five years. God, how he needed a vacation! He looked up just as his partner, Gabe Nexs, walked into the squad room. "Morning, Bobby" grumbled Gabe.

"Mornin', Gabe. How's it treating you so far?"

"Fuck, man. First thing this morning, my coffee machine craps out on me, then a pipe bursts in my bathroom. Life is just fucking peachy!" Bobby listened with laughter in his eyes. He had liked Gabe since the first time they met. He always made Bobby's problems seem so insignificant not that he really had time for problems; after all, all he did was work and sleep and eat when time permitted. Except for weekends, when Hailey made him come over for supper, he never ate healthy food. He had met Hailey about three years earlier during an investigation into a homicide. She was digging up information on some chump who had split with over three grand worth of rare coins, stolen from some eighty year old rich cracker who decided he could hire some street trash to help him take care of his estate. In the end, the trash just ripped him off and he ended up with a bullet hole between his eyes. Bobby had ended up having to question Hailey about it, and ever since they'd been best buddies. Which reminded him that he was supposed to meet her for lunch. "What's on the list for today, Bobby?" Gabe asked while stirring his coffee and shuffling papers around his desk.

"Not much. Captain isn't in yet so I haven't really thought about work yet."

"So ..." Gabe took a sip of his coffee. "... what have you been thinking about?" he asked with a mischievous look in his eye. "Not anything kinky about a certain female PI perhaps?" Bobby didn't even twitch at that comment; Gabe had always ridden him about his friendship with Hailey. He never could grasp that a man could just be friends with a beautiful woman. "No, I was not thinking about Hailey at all actually. I was thinking about my vacation I've got coming to me."

"Oh yeah? Where you planning on going Bobby?"

"I'm not too sure yet. I'm thinking of Australia."

"Man, I would love to just take off where no one could find me," Gabe said with a smirk on his face. Bobby, knowing his partner, looked at him and just started to laugh. "Yeah, right! I know you; you wouldn't go anywhere. You'd just hole up in some dingy little shit-hole with some broad who couldn't even spell her own name." Laughing also, Gabe just nodded but decided to flip him the bird just because it was Bobby.

*   *   *   *

"Goddamn sons a' bitches!" Grabbing a wrench, Hailey had an incredible urge to beat the living snot out of the driver's seat as payback for pinching her finger but instead beat the cement floor, chipping off pieces in the process. Looking at her watch, she stood and stretched the kinks out, sighing, just realizing how hungry she was and how late it was getting. After cleaning up her tools, she bent down and decided to try one more time with the driver's seat, being careful to keep her fingers from getting pinched again. "Well, would you look at that!" Laughing to herself, she got up and stared admiringly at her own handi work. Her baby was finally done. "Great job, Hailey!" she shouted to herself as she jogged up to the house to shower and change. If she didn't hurry, she was going to be late, and Bobby was always riding on her about time. She never understood his fascination with time, considering he was usually the late one. Hailey couldn't wait till Bobby saw the car. He always wanted to help her with it, but she was dead set against it. She felt that if he helped her, then it wouldn't feel like her baby. Besides, he wouldn't have known what to do anyway; mental work was more his style than manual. Stripping as she walked, she picked up her phone and called Bobby at work.

"Mercer Police Station, how may I direct your call?"

"Bobby Stein's desk, please. It's Hailey Velck calling."

"Just a moment."

"Stein." He barked into the receiver.

"What crawled up your ass?"

"How's it going?"

"Great so far. Just on my way into the shower. I was calling to say that I'm picking you up but you're paying." Bobby chuckled. "Sure thing, and I'm inviting Gabe." They hung up, and Hailey cranked some "TNT" by AC/DC and hopped into the shower.

*   *   *   *

After easing the dark metallic blue Mustang out of the garage, she turned on to her street and glided to Mercer Way. She headed for the station. Bobby was going to be surprised to see the car. The last time he'd seen it, it was just the frame with all its parts spread around.

The car was running smoothly; she shifted into third and glided down the street then shifted down and spun into the Mercer Police Station parking lot. She spotted the captain and hit the horn while backing into a spot.

"Finally finished the car? Looks beautiful!" She got out and grinned, running her hand over the hood. "Thanks. Shall we go in, Jeremy?" They walked in and up the stairs to the homicide unit. Gabe glanced up at the sound of the door swishing.

"Hey, Stein. Looks like the captain is in. Check out the dish on his arm!" Bobby looked up, "Shut-up Nexs. It's just Hailey. Hey, Cap. How's it hanging?"

"Detectives. Nexs why are you grinning like an idiot?"

"He is an idiot, sir." Gabe turned and punched Bobby in the arm. The captain headed to his office, and the trio headed for the door. "Where are we eating today?"

"I figured Al Boccalino's. Everyone okay with that?" The guys grunted.

"You finished the car! Looks awesome!" She was sure she saw a little bit of envy in his eyes. "Thanks. After three years, it had better look good." They all climbed in with Gabe in the back seat. Gabe looked around the interior and sighed. He wished he had the time or the brains to rebuild something like this, or build anything actually. "You fit back there, Gabe? Not too cramped?" In a gruff voice, he replied, "Not a bad fit if I do say so myself, and I do, but I was wondering if we were almost there?" Hailey chuckled, "Just pulling in." She parked, and they piled out and into Hailey's favorite restaurant. She loved Al's. She made sure to come at least twice a week and usually with Bobby. They were considered the best of customers and usually Al himself would join them for a glass of the house wine. Looking around, she felt the warmth and friendly feeling that every square inch of the room radiated. She smiled, and in that moment, a tall, burly man appeared in front of them.

"Hailey! Bobby! Wonderful to look at you two. It's been too long since you step into my restaurant!" He gathered them both up into a giant bear hug. "I was just here a week ago," Hailey responded. Introductions were made to Gabe. "Pleasure to meet you, sir. I'm looking forward to eating some of the great Italian food that these two have so often praised!"

"Of course! Of course! Right this way. I have perfect spot. It has wonderful view of street, and you can smell the wondrous aromas floating from kitchen.

I join shortly for glass of wine on me. Enjoy!" He smiled and scurried away, no doubt to make sure they got the best of service.

*   *   *   *

The breeze was blowing swiftly but smoothly over Lake Washington, and the sun, to everyone's delight, was radiating pleasant warmth. Burrows Landing Park was littered with families and their pets. Amongst the trees by the beach, Rye and Mocca lay enjoying the view. "A lot of sailboats out today," Rye commented. Mocca huffed in reply, bringing Rye's hand to her head automatically.

Rye had found Mocca in a cardboard box on the side of the road when she was only a few months old. He had kept her hidden for a few days from his parents but by then, she had some of her strength back and wouldn't stay in his room any longer. One morning, his mother had woken up to Mocca licking her nose and almost had a heart attack. Rye had gotten some intense ear chewing, first for bringing a dog into the house and second for not telling them for three days. Ever since then, Mocca and Rye had been inseparable.

"Well, girl, shall we grab a couple of hot dogs and walk along the beach?" Rye stood and hooked the leash to Mocca's collar, scratched behind her ear, and gathered his hat and sunglasses. They strolled over to the hot-dog man where Rye bought two dogs, one with sauerkraut and the other with mustard and sweet relish, and placed the sauerkraut dog in front of Mocca who devoured it in two licks. Strolling along the warm sand watching the sailboats glide across the lake, Rye and Mocca headed for the car. Once home, Rye placed fresh water on the floor for Mocca and then headed for the shower. Exiting his bedroom, he was drying his hair with a towel when he stumbled over Mocca and slammed into the fridge. "Fuck!" Rubbing his shoulder, he opened the fridge and grabbed a Corona then headed for the sun deck placing some Ozzie on the stereo as he walked by.

Leaning against the railing, he gazed out across the lake and surveyed the serene vista wishing he hadn't sold his sailboat last year. Rye was thirty-two with a well-proportioned, beautifully defined body. He carried his six-foot-four-inch frame with dignified grace around Chesterfield Park every morning at 5:00am. Usually, the sun would be flooding and weaving through the tall spruces, kissing his skin, as he left the shadows of the trees. His hair was sandy and unkempt. Behind his wire-framed glasses, captivating gray eyes freckled with emerald green specks, gazed purposefully into whatever he was working on.

His home was a split-level with cedar flooring and a light husky blue stone coloring on the walls. He had had his home rebuilt in loft fashion with the open upper level and the spiral stairs. His living room was littered with books and model cars amongst his dark maroon furniture. It was a very comfortable and cozy room with a deep-set fireplace embedded in the far wall, opposite the television and stereo equipment. The walls were lined with a smoky-colored wallpaper border that blended well with the stone washed walls.

His kitchen was spacious and bright with overhead skylights and spotlights strategically placed to illuminate every inch of the kitchen. All his appliances were chrome. There was gray tiling on the floor and counters. When he was able to cook, which was rare, he liked to do so in style.

The sun deck was connected to the kitchen that directly faced the west side of the lake. His bedroom was filled with dark greens and blues, which emitted subtle signs of masculinity. The room was furnished with a canopy bed fashioned in rough black iron and old English-style accessories. There was an old, late Renaissance, Victorian-style desk under the window overlooking the lake and an old grandfather clock beside it. An adjoining bathroom, which he colored in blues with hints of white, was styled with an old-claw foot tub that he had remodeled to help accommodate the shower. It stood along the far wall with an old-fashioned toilet at the opposite end. The sink was one of those tall porcelain types with the big taps.

Mocca's room was colored in browns just a shade darker than her coloring and was located on the lower level by the kitchen. There wasn't much in this room except her bed, water, and food bowl and a few chew toys that she loved to hide in Rye's bedding. The room used to be used as a storage room but Mocca always slept in it, so Rye converted it into her pen. Coming in from the deck, Rye was stopped by the jangle of the telephone.

"Hello?"

"Doctor Jackson?"

"Yes, this is he."

"Hi. My name is Sara, Sara Connel. I'm related to Mike Connel?"

"Oh yes. I'm glad you called. I'm assuming someone has contacted you from my office? Well, I just thought you should know that Mike was brought in last night and that he was not murdered, as there was some speculation. He died of self-inflicted wounds to the throat and abdomen."

"Where was he found, Dr. Jackson?"

"He was found in his apartment at his kitchen table. Is there anything you can tell me about his state of mind recently?"

"Not really. I mean, my family has kind of disowned him because he got really heavy into the drugs and drinking, so I haven't really talked to him much."

"Okay, well, if you would like him back for burial, just contact my office and they can arrange for pick-up when you like or the city can take care of it for you."

"Umm … I'm not too sure what I want to do. I think I would like to call my family before I say anything. Is that okay?"

"Of course, Ms. Connel. Like I said, just call my office and tell them what you would like to do. Thanks for calling, and I'm sorry for your loss. Good day, Ms. Connel." Hanging up, Rye let out a deep sigh thensat down on the sofa. He turned off the stereo and clicked on the television, surfing through the channels but not really paying attention to what was flashing by as he thought about work. Mike Connel's body had come in around 2:00am. His neck had been punctured at the jugular and a deep incision had pierced his main artery in the lower body. Needless to say, Mike had been dead for a week before anyone had complained about his television being cranked for days. Mocca, sensing her master was thinking about work, came trotting over to him and placed her head in his lap, bringing him back to the present.

"Hello, girl."

Mocca huffed in reply and nudged Rye's hand onto her head. Rye gladly obliged and started to scratch behind each ear while watching the daily news. The reporter was standing in front of the Overview Medical Center talking about some woman who had apparently been found just moments before on the steps of the mayor's office. Rye just sighed and mumbled to himself, "Well, I guess I'm going to work today after all," and not a minute later, he heard the jangle of his telephone.

*   *   *   *

"Good of you to come in, Doctor," Mayor Manny Cross said to Rye without rising from behind his desk. Manny Cross was a tall man in his mid-fifties with silver hair and a perfect tan. Rye disliked him immensely. He found Manny to be a very arrogant and obtrusive man, not to mention obnoxious as all hell. Unfortunately for Rye however, whenever he beckoned, he had to oblige and come to his aid. "From the looks of the victim," the mayor's adviser started, "she was brutally attacked."

"No kidding? Maybe that's why you guys called me in." Rye replied with a look focused at the adviser. "Now, Doctor, let's not be sarcastic. If we all get along, this will be a lot easier to figure out. The main thing here is: who killed her and why was she dumped on my steps?" Manny stated with authority. "Let's call Jeremy Piper in with his best."

CHAPTER 2

As they were arriving at the station, Bobby's and Gabe's beepers both went off. "Sounds like you boys got some work to do," Hailey commented with humor in her voice. Bobby smiled and said, "Well, hopefully, we'll get to call you in for help!"

"You just forget that thought, Bobby Lewis Stein, or I'll personally break every one of your toes! By the way, thanks for lunch and great seeing you again, Gabe. Now off to work." She sped away and left them both standing there in a cloud of dust and exhaust.

Inside the station, in the homicide unit, it was all chaos. Detective Zurk spotted Bobby and Gabe and yelled, "Hey, boys! Captain wants you both in his office pronto!" Waving their thanks, they strolled over to the captain's door and knocked. "Get in here!" yelled the captain. "Where the hell have you two been? It's been over an hour."

"We were having lunch with Hailey, Captain. Sorry we took so long. What's up?" Bobby inquired while Gabe went and stood over by the window watching the street with minor attention. "The mayor called me with very upsetting news. Apparently, they found a young woman naked and very much dead on the steps of the mayor's office. He called me to get my best men on the job so that's where you two come in." Gabe looked over at the captain with a grin. "Why, thanks, Cap! It is true; we are your best. So what's the plan?"

"You two are to go and meet the mayor and Dr. Rye Jackson over at Overview Medical now. Report back to me with details." They left the captain's office and headed for the station parking lot. "Man was he ever pissy! He was just fine an hour ago. The mayor must be really busting his ass." Bobby looked over at his partner and replied, "The mayor is always riding everyone's ass, dip-shit; that's why he's the mayor." Bobby and Gabe arrived at the hospital and went directly to the morgue where they met up with the mayor. "Gentlemen, hello. Sorry to have to meet you this way, but I'm told I've got nothing but the best, and I demand the best. This here is Dr. Rye Jackson. He's one of the leading medical examiners for the city. I want the three of you to establish what transpired with that young woman and who the hell did it. I'll leave it to you men, but I want updates." He turned and exited the room leaving the three of them standing there. "What an asshole!" Bobby murmured, and Gabe grunted. "I'm sure glad to know we're all in agreement," Rye commented with a grin and reached out to take Bobby's and Gabe's hands. "I know we all know each other here, so I'll just get on with the autopsy. It's not a very pleasant scene in there, so you are now forewarned. Follow me." Stepping into the autopsy room, Bobby had to take a deep breath at the sight of what lay on the table. Rye quickly pulled on a sterile face guard and latex gloves then handed two to Bobby and Gabe. He then proceeded to gather the necessary tools to examine the body in detail. The woman, who couldn't have been older than twenty-eight, had once been very beautiful, but now she was a repulsive mass of blood, bone, and tissue. With a quick glance at the body, Bobby knew, in his gut, that this killer was just beginning. The victim's face had been badly beaten, and where the eyes should have been, there was nothing but two charred holes. Her neck had rope-burn marks on every inch and what appeared to be traces of a dark cloth embedded in the burns. The chest cavity had been savagely ripped open, causing the flesh to hang in ribbons, but the heart had been removed with clean and precise cuts. The rest of the body had not been molested, but both wrists and ankles showed signs of restraint.

As Rye examined the body, Bobby grunted into his cell phone and frowned. The prints they lifted weren't on direct file. The body on the table was another Jane Doe. He slapped his phone shut and stalked over to Gabe and Rye. It upset him when the loss of a life, especially one so young and beautiful, required investigation into the reasons it happened and who did it.

Gabe looked over at Bobby and noticing his scowl said, "Hey, man, what's got you?" Bobby looked up from the body and motioned for Gabe to follow. "Doc, call me on my cell, number is 261-6778, if you find anything else we should know about." Leaving the room, Bobby pulled out a smoke and headed for the car. "What's going on?" He didn't say anything, just kept walking till they reached the car. "Anything in there remind you of something?" Gabe narrowed his eyes and scratched his head. "No, I don't think so.

Why?" Bobby started the car and turned to look at Gabe. "It bears close resemblance to a serial murder about six years back. I wasn't on the case then, I was still a rookie, but everyone heard about it. All the victims had their hearts removed." Gabe sat in thought for a moment. "Well, that victim had her eyes burnt out and her heart removed. Do you think it's connected? Could just be a coincidence."

"That's true, but they never did catch the guy. They came very close, but he evaded them and there were no more murders. The fuckin' reporters called him 'Broken Heart.' Well, we're going to catch this fucker and soon." When they returned to the station, Gabe went directly to his desk and picked up the phone but Bobby went to the file room and collected every piece of information on the murders that happened six years ago and took them back to his desk.

*   *   *   *

Hailey was sitting in her office drinking tea and going over last-minute details on her latest case. She loved her job. Even when some of her cases were just wives hiring her to spy on their husbands and their lovers, like the case she was working on now. It happened about two weeks ago. Hailey had been tidying up her office when this little woman came in. She had told Hailey about how she was having suspicions about her husband getting mixed up in something illegal and cheating on her. She had asked Hailey to investigate for a very modest fee, Hailey was very interested, so three days later, she found herself outside a very dingy-looking motel spying on a Mr. Brochell and some twenty-year-old bimbo. Anyway, the lady was coming in today, and Hailey had a lot to tell her.

Two hours later while Hailey was sitting on her deck drinking strawberry tea, Mrs. Brochell walked into the office. "Hello? Hailey?" Hearing her name, she yelled, "Out here!" Mary Brochell glided out onto the deck and sat beside Hailey, helping herself to some tea. "Mary! Good to see you again. Unfortunately, it had to be under these circumstances."

"Yes, it is a shame we couldn't talk about something pleasant, but I am worried about this situation." Hailey studied the little woman sitting beside her. "I know you are, and I just want to say that I'm sorry for that. Anyway, on to business." Hailey leaned over and picked up the file and handed it to Mary. She sat there, quiet, waiting for Mary to read through it. Ten minutes later, Mary sat back in the chair and stared out over the lake. "That son of a bitch. What should I do?" They faced each other, and Hailey said, "I don't know if my opinion counts, but I'd divorce his ass and get his little-money laundering business busted. I know a great lawyer, good friend of mine. Owes me a few favors. I'll call him if you want. He'll help you out for a good price." Standing, Mrs. Brochell turned and shook Hailey's hand. "No. That's okay. I have a very close friend who can help me out, but thank you very much." Mary Brochell paid Hailey, threw the file into her bag, and left. Hailey got up and went inside to her desk. After picking up the 'Brochell' file and filing it away, she went upstairs for some dinner.

*   *   *   *

"Bobby! Got a lead on the Jane Doe. Her name is Sheila Voice. Worked at some little coffee joint off of Washington Street." Bobby threw the file he was reading on his desk and grabbed his jacket and cell. He and Gabe ran out the door. "Her boss said that she hasn't been in to work for a few days and that isn't at all like her." Gabe grabbed the keys out of Bobby's hand and got into the driver's seat. Bobby, slightly annoyed, unwillingly got into the passenger seat and asked Gabe where he found the info on their Jane Doe. Gabe said that he had made a few calls to a couple of his contacts and hit pay dirt. Someone had also called from the ME's office with a positive ID on the body. It wasn't every day that Gabe's contacts came through. Most of the time, they fed him lines of bullshit, and he always fell for it. Sometimes, Bobby worried about him. Gabe had a tendency to believe whatever people told him. He was a bit naive when it came to matters of a serious nature. It was ironic actually, considering he was a cop, but Bobby knew some people were just born that way. After pulling into the parking lot of the coffee shop, both detectives put on their game faces and headed in.

Suzie was working the counter when she saw two of the sexiest men walk through the door; she almost dropped the coffeepot right on her foot. She watched as they each grabbed a stool and scoped out the place. "Welcome, guys! What can I get you?" Suzie stood there with a grin from ear to ear, her hip cocked to one side and the three top buttons of her blouse undone so as to show off her voluptuous chest, hoping these two beautiful men would take notice and start hitting on her. Suzie badly wanted to get married, but every guy she had gone out with lately had turned into a major loser. Gabe, recognizing her flirtatious signals, was chatting her up while Bobby sat and waited for the owner to come and talk to him. Surveying the coffee shop, he noticed a short, stout man rumbling his way towards him. Using his cop sense, he made an assessment of this man and came up with a few details only his trained eye would find. He determined that this man would try his hardest to evade all important questions and try to shift the focus mainly onto himself. He was highly self-absorbed. He also struck Bobby as a very arrogant and self-centered man who probably always tried to take home his hired help. Bobby hoped that he didn't give him the run-around because he just was not in the mood. "You must be Detective Stein. Hello. I'm Matt Penguin." Mr. Penguin pulled up a stool beside Bobby and signaled to the flirty waitress. "Mary Sue! Coffee." Once she had brought his coffee and refilled Bobby's, he suggested that they go somewhere private, Bobby introduced Gabe as the detective who talked to him on the phone. "Well gentlemen, how about we go into that booth behind us? It'll be a little more private for us." Sliding into the booth, Bobby pulled out his pad and pen and asked the first question. "Mr. Penguin, what can you tell us about Sheila Voice?" Watching him, they both noticed his sudden shift of attention and the glaze over his eyes. "Sheila. She was a very pretty young lady with beautiful green eyes that seemed like they sparkled every time she smiled. She was always full of energy, you know what I mean? It's like she was just in love with life and everyone around and involved with her. She could make the saddest person laugh with delight at the simplest of things. I really cared for her. Everyone here loved working with her and most of my customers only came here because of her." Matt took a sip of his coffee and just stared at the table. Gabe and Bobby exchanged glances and went on with the questioning. "So you don't remember any one person coming in here and paying an extreme amount of attention to Sheila?" Matt stared at the table for a few minutes longer and then glanced at both detectives and said, "No, I don't, but Mary Sue might remember. She got to know Sheila pretty well." Gabe's eyes lit up at the mention of the cute waitress so Bobby told him that he could handle that line of questioning. While Gabe went over to talk to Mary Sue, Bobby asked Matt a few more questions about Sheila and her work performance.

CHAPTER 3

Back at the morgue, Rye was examining Sheila's body from head to toe with a tape recorder in hand. "The body is about five feet ten inches long and has a little tattoo of a rose near the collar bone. Body has been dead for approximately three weeks. Her face has been beaten with a large, blunt weapon seeming to resemble a club of some sort, made up of wood. Have taken several splinters about three inches in length from wounds in face. Eyes have been burnt out with a very hot, thin iron pole. Have found iron residue around eye sockets. Skin area around throat is badly burned from cloth restraints. Removed six pieces of a dark material from several burns on her throat. Moving to chest area. Chest cavity has been ripped open with what looks like hands, too sloppy to be anything else. Examining ribs and surrounding area. All soft tissue has been ripped, causing flesh to hang in ribbons, confirming statement before stated. Ribs have been broken manually. Heart is missing. Suspect removed heart with proper and clean incisions made to arteries and veins. Replaced heart with what looks to be a white lily. Moving down lower torso reveals no injury to legs, but ankles have been bound with same material as found in neck wounds. Wrists have also been bound with same material. Will roll body on to the left side to examine backside. Back of head is in tact. Back has no wounds except a small incision in the lower area, near the right hip. Area is hard around incision suggesting embedment." He reached over and picked up very slim and long tweezers, and began extracting a small object fixed into the incision. "Using tweezers to remove object. A small piece of paper with a short message found inside. Message reads, 'Gathering abundance brings peace to mind. I will collect those that prove to be of pure heart to cleanse myself of all impurities.' Rest of body is intact. End of oral exam." Rye gathered up all of the evidence and sent the pieces of cloth to the lab to be tested but placed the note into a baggy and the white lily into a clear, plastic container. He picked up the phone and dialed Bobby's cell number while arranging his thoughts. He figured Bobby would be quite surprised and a little disturbed about all that he had found. "Stein here."

"Hello. Dr. Jackson here. You asked me to call if I found anything interesting."

"Yes? I take it you found something?" Rye sat down at his desk and gathered up the container holding the flower. "Yeah, you could say that. I would rather talk about it in person, though, so if you could please come to my office as soon as possible …"

"Sure thing, Doc. We'll wrap it up here and be there in an hour."

"See you then, Detective."

*   *   *   *

Hailey was just sitting down to dinner when her phone rang. Every instinct told her to ignore it, but she answered anyway. After all, she knew it was Bobby. "Hey." She sat cradling the phone between her shoulder and cheek and continued to cut up her steak while listening to Bobby cuss and yell at some driver who had just cut him off. "Hey, Hailey. Interrupt you at anything?"

"Yeah, you did. Just sat down to eat a nice, fat, juicy steak. What do you want?" She took a bite and moaned in pleasure, knowing Bobby was drooling. "Damn, girl! Why don't you ever cook steak when I'm over for dinner?"

"I don't like to share my steak, especially when it's prime-grade New York steak, baby. Besides, you love my pasta." Smirking, she poured herself some more red wine and took a slow swallow. She much preferred red to white wine, because it was always richer and sweeter and she loved the feel of it sliding down her throat. "Well, sorry for the interruption, but I'll make it quick. I was wondering if you'd be interested in some leg work for me soon? I've got a situation forming, and I could use some out-of-force help, if you get my meaning." He fell silent and waited for her answer. Hailey, meanwhile, was savoring her meal and thinking about sky-diving. "Well Bobby … I could be persuaded, if you took me out one night for some fun. I'm getting kind of antsy this month. I need to cut loose and groove. Get some guys together and pick a date."

"Ahhh, Christ, Hailey! I hate dancing, and you know it. But fine, how about this Saturday? Now tomorrow, come to the station around 11:00am, and I'll fill you in. Thanks, babe. Talk to you later." Bobby hung up before she could answer.

Damn him! she thought. She'd give him a piece of her mind tomorrow but right now, she was going to finish her meal, then go soak in the tub while listening to 'Diana Krall'.

Hailey's living room was a large, comfortable space with dark cedar paneling covering the walls from floor to ceiling. Her furniture was over-sized and a smoky rust color. Her couch and armchair were smothered in down-filled cushions and pillows. It was furniture that grabbed you as you entered the room and held you, hugging your body until you were fighting sleep. In a pile were two enormous beanbag chairs in an army-style camouflage pattern. A few freestanding lamps illuminated the cozy living room with a soft, warm glow. Candles placed around the room helped to achieve this welcoming gentle radiance. On cold nights, the warmth came from the fireplace, which was embedded in the east wall. It had a charcoal slate hearth, outlined in a rough slate brick. Her favorite reading chair was placed off to the side but still in the path of the embracing warmth emitted by the fire. Hailey loved reading by the soft light from a kerosene lamp scented with a light vanilla. She also had several dignified candles on the solid oak end table beside the chair. In the center of the room was the matching oak coffee table with vibrantly green ivy, covering the entire thing like a knit blanket. Two of the walls had large, thick pine shelves filled with tons of hard-cover books, covering about almost everything a person would need to know for whatever reason. The other shelves held model cars from every year, every make and model. The kitchen was spacious with vaulted ceilings and walls the color of lemon sherbet. The counters were uncluttered, broken up only by the necessary shiny appliances shoved in the corners and stylish dry ingredient canisters. White marble counters outlined in a forest-green tile back splash made the kitchen feel clean and fresh. A small island stood in the center of the kitchen with copper pots and pans hanging above. The sink was located about one stride away from the island, directly in front of a bay window, giving Hailey a perfect spot to grow herbs and a beautiful view of the lake, especially in the early evening when the sun slowly sank behind the buildings across the water, making the city appear to be engulfed in flames. Then as quickly as the flames died out, the moon rose higher and higher sending a chilling sparkle across the still, rippling water. Hailey's bedroom was furnished with very simple but striking furniture. The bed was king-sized with a huge down-filled duvet billowing on top of it in a light-cream-and-blue checkered pattern. The closet was open faced and crammed with every type of clothing one would need for any situation and all types of foot-wear. Her dresser was a black rod iron with mahogany accents. Two of the drawers were filled with miscellaneous items while the other four were filled with everyday clothing, like Levi's 501 jeans, t-shirts, and sweatshirts. Most of the sweatshirts were either a black or dark navy in color, due to her routine. In the corner of the room was a cushy-looking chair with a satin nightgown draped over the back and a black leather jacket tossed haphazardly over the arm, creating just the right amount of attitude to her room.

*   *   *   *

At 11:30 am, Hailey found herself perched on Bobby's desk with a sugar-coated dough-nut in one hand and a cup of coffee in the other, while Bobby filled her in on the case. "The victim's name is Shelia Voice, twenty-five years of age, no priors. Family's dead, and she moved here about two years ago. She worked at a little coffee shop off of Washington called ..." He shuffled a few papers around and came up with the name. "The Saucer." Hailey sat there for a moment, finished her coffee, threw the cup away, and then focused on Bobby. "And what would you like me to dig up?"

"Gabe and I interviewed the owner and one of the waitresses, so I'd like you to check out her place and streets. Try to find some of her friends. Infiltrate the hangouts. Isn't that what you call it?" he asked, cocking an eyebrow. He was always trying to get Hailey to talk about that part of her past. She was always so closed about it ... well some of it anyway. All she ever told him was that some of it she would rather not talk about. Bobby always got mad when she said that. "What about the killer? Anything on him or her yet?" Hailey asked. "Nothing yet ... except, and this is just my opinion, the killer has a very fucked-up head. The victim had her eyes burnt out and her chest ripped open with her heart removed." Bobby sat back and placed his hands behind his head, watching her. Most women he knew would cringe at what he had just told her but not Hailey. She just closed up, showing no emotion. He couldn't even read her eyes. "I'll see what I can do. I'll be in touch." She stood, threw a grin at Bobby, and left the station.

*   *   *   *

Back at her office, Hailey grabbed a mug of tea and sat in front of her computer. Her morning meeting with Bobby was definitely not what she had had in mind. Hailey didn't mind helping Bobby out. After all, it was a little bit more cash and she didn't work for free even for Bobby, but she really hated the nature of the case not to mention the trouble Bobby could get into if his captain found out he had brought in a civilian. The main reason Hailey left the service was to get away from the brutish displays of humankind at its worst. Sometimes, she wished the world was one peaceful place and nobody had to worry about death and destruction. Sorting the particulars of the case in her head, she assembled the facts from the file Bobby had let her read and placed her concentration on the autopsy. Hailey knew one thing about death; it always had a tale to tell. She powered up her computer, opened her notebook, and started jotting down numbers and thoughts. Recalling the coroner's office number, she picked up the phone and dialed.

"Coroner's office," a bored voice spoke out. "I'd like to speak to Dr. Jackson, please," Hailey said with a slight urgency in her tone. Silence followed, then she heard what she classified as elevator music coming from the receiver then the bored voice again. "Sorry. Dr. Jackson isn't taking calls at the moment."

"Tell him it's in reference to the Shelia Voice autopsy."

"Hang on." Elevator music again. "Dr. Jackson here." Hailey's breath hitched at the voice flowing to her ear. It was slightly husky, running over her senses like melted chocolate. She cleared her throat. "Hi. Ah, I'm not sure if Detective Stein got in touch with you yet, but I'm Hailey Velck, a private investigator helping out on the case, and I was wondering if I'd be able to come talk to you and examine the body myself?" Hailey bit her lower lip in frustration, waiting for his response. "Yes, Ms. Velck. He contacted me, and I would definitely be willing to talk with you. When is good for you?"

"Tomorrow, around one pm?"

"Sounds good. See you then." Hailey hung up the phone and took a deep breath. She hadn't felt these emotions for the opposite sex in a very long time, and she was getting excited to meet Rye tomorrow. Until then, though, she decided she would start checking on line for missing children and maybe even some chat rooms. She might get lucky.

CHAPTER 4

Meanwhile, back at the station, Bobby and Gabe were pouring over the old case file hoping to find some sort of clue and maybe even a connection that Bobby was sure was there. The only differences in the cases were the white lily, the burning of the eyes and the note left in the body. Everything else was the same. It made Bobby cringe sometimes, how evil mankind could be. He was glad he'd brought Hailey into it, because she could get into places Gabe and he couldn't, and he felt that there was more to this case than the naked eye could see. Slamming the file closed, Bobby stood up and began to pace. "What's up?" Gabe asked while stretching his big, bulky frame and tugging on his "lumber-jack" beard. "There's something tugging on the back of my mind about the victim. We can't find anything of her life, and what we do have ... it fuckin' doesn't tell us very much. I know there's something more to her, and for the life of me, I can't figure it out." He stopped and grabbed the back of his chair and stared out the window while Gabe sat in silence for a moment. "Maybe Hailey will dig up more info for us? She usually comes through."

"Yeah. She usually does, but I know she isn't exactly excited to do this for us."

"How do you know?" Gabe asked with his brow creased. "I could tell by the way she completely closed up. She has that talent for wiping all her emotions off her face. That's how I can tell that she really didn't want to do the case." Bobby went to the coffee machine and poured himself a cup of the hot, dark sludge. "Then why is she?" Gabe asked with the sincerity of a three-year-old asking why he can't pull the dog's tail. "She's doing it because Hailey doesn't back down from anything." Bobby threw the coffee cup away and walked to the locker room to shower.

"Nexs!" Gabe swiveled his chair around to see what the yelling was about. "Got a 187 over at Dearborn Park. Cap said you and Stein get it."

"Got it, Parker," Gabe grumbled while he grabbed his jacket and went to get Bobby.

18

*   *   *   *

Arriving at the scene, Bobby immediately took charge and went straight for the body, taking in everything on his way. Gabe went to the first officer in blue he saw and sent her to do crowd control while he scanned it for any street face that might talk to him. One thing he'd learned in this line of work was that most street people liked to talk to cash. No one popped out at him. He walked over to his partner and studied him while he examined the victim. He jotted down information that was being fed to him from the officer who called it in. Standing, Bobby lit a cigar. "Looks to be the same M-O, like the last victim. Same height and build and probably age too. Hair color's even the same. No identification or clothing, eyes burned out and chest ripped open with heart removed, and I'd bet my bottom dollar that there's even a little note from the killer." He took a long drag from the cigar while waiting for Gabe's two cents worth. "Guess we got ourselves a vicious wacko who wants an audience," Gabe replied with a sneer spreading across his mouth. Bobby stomped out the cigar and responded, "Better call in the cavalry then." He walked to the car to call in forensics.

An hour later, the forensic team arrived and quickly went to work. Tommy Paparille, senior forensics leader and Bobby's poker-playing buddy, walked over to chat. "Damn shame to be called out tonight." Tommy pulled out a pack of Benson and Hedges and lit up. "What's the story?" Bobby leaned on the hood of the car and watched the team in action before answering. "All I know so far is same MO as the last except the place. Female, between the ages of twenty and thirty, blond hair, and slim in build. I'm guessing time of death was around seven in the morning just after the morning jog rush." Tommy was quiet, taking it all in, Bobby imagined, but it didn't make him any less patient. "Well, I guess we'll have our work cut out for us then, and we'll have to post-pone the next few poker games till this mess is cleaned up." He stomped out his smoke and headed over to the crime scene. Bobby couldn't help himself and grinned despite the situation. It never failed to amaze him how Tommy could always find the humor in everything. He pushed off the car and strolled over to where Gabe stood in what looked to be a very intense discussion. "Nexs." At the sound of his name, Gabe swirled around and Bobby saw the anger burning in his eyes. "Easy, man, it's just me. What's got you so riled up?" Gabe took a deep breath to calm himself down and answered, "This yahoo," throwing his thumb over his shoulder at the journalist who was drilling daggers in his back with his eyes, "wants me to let him over the line and give him an interview. Says he has chief's approval." Bobby bit his lip to suppress the grin tugging at his mouth and placed his arm around Gabe's shoulders giving them privacy. "Bullshit he does! Listen, this is what we'll do …" Bobby slapped Gabe on the shoulder, and he shrugged and turned around. "What's your name and what paper you work for?" The journalist looked up and grinned, "Name's James Tracker, work for the Herald." Gabe stared at him with hard gray eyes. "You write that article on that heist at the bank?" James' smile grew, and he nodded enthusiastically. Gabe grinned at Bobby and then motioned to the journalist. "Follow me." He brought him over to a street cop and sent them off on false interviews. Gabe turned around to Bobby with a gleam in his eye. "Sent them off looking for an old lady with supposed information regarding this." He motioned with his hand around them. "What are you two grinning about? This is hardly the time." Bobby and Gabe both jumped and spun around to see Hailey standing not two feet behind them with her hands on her hips and glancing from one to the other. "Ahhh … nothing." They both wiped the grins off, and Gabe turned and busied himself with finding witnesses. "What was that all about?" Hailey turned to Bobby and waited for a reply. Bobby just shook his head and motioned for her to follow him. When she got the call from Bobby to come down, she had been searching futilely for several hours on-line for anything concerning runaways or lost young women with no luck at all. "What's the story, Bobby?" Hailey crouched down next to the victim examining with her eyes and being sure to stay out of the team's way. "Well … so far, it looks like the same killer. Her age is unknown, but I'd bet she's about twenty to thirty years of age, very fit, and was once very beautiful. Other than that, we haven't found much." He watched her examine the body and was once again relieved that he had brought her onto the team. "Hailey … I just wanted to tell you how much I appreciate you agreeing to work on this with Gabe and me. I know how much you hate seeing wasted life." Hailey continued to study the body. She heard every word he had said to her and she was glad he'd said it, but she would not answer him. "Has the forensics team taken pictures of the body yet?" She glanced over her shoulder at him. "Not sure. I'll ask Tommy." He sauntered off towards Tommy, and Hailey sat back on her heels. She wanted to know if the team had taken pictures of the body, because she had noticed some small, light scars located on the victim's lower body and she wanted copies. She had a feeling there were more, and she wanted to make sure she could have a look at the body once it was transported to the morgue. She noticed that the victim's mouth was left untouched and closed. She stood up and walked to Bobby's car, opened the trunk, and removed a set of latex gloves. Pulling them on, she walked back to the body and knelt down beside it, gently pulling down the lower jaw. Inside the victim's mouth, she found a small piece of paper and a missing tongue. Unfolding the paper, she read the message, "One is done; two will be through. Pure of heart is to be true." She was placing the note into an evidence bag as, Bobby returned and squatted beside her. "Whatcha got there?" Without looking over at him, Hailey handed him the bag. "It's a piece of paper. Looks like the killer left a message. I found it stuffed inside the victim's mouth ... and by the way, the tongue is missing." She stood up to stretch her legs, and Bobby followed suit.

"Tommy said that they're finished with the body so if you want me to get it transported, I'll make the call." Hailey just nodded and continued to stare at the body. "So young. Where's her tongue and her heart? The first victim, was her tongue missing?" Now she turned and headed towards Bobby's car with him beside her, matching her stride. "I thought you examined the other body?"

"I haven't gotten a chance to go there yet. I was on my way, but then you called me so I came straight here."

"The other victim had her tongue, but we did find a note. It was stuffed in a little incision on her lower back. Rye will show you. I'm calling him now." They reached the car, and Bobby pulled out his cell and dialed the doctor. Hailey rested against the car, waiting.

CHAPTER 5

Arriving at the morgue with the latest victim, Hailey followed the gurney into the exam room. The young attendant, Hailey thought his name was Sean, introduced her to Dr. Jackson. After Sean left and the pleasantries were done with, they began to examine the body. "Sorry I didn't make it earlier, but Bobby called me on my way here, so I thought I'd pop over there before I came here, seeing as it was another murder." Rye straightened and looked over at her. He had expected something different than what she was. Hearing her over the phone had not prepared him for what he saw. Bobby had told him she was beautiful, but what Rye saw wasn't just beautiful but goddamn sexy and very intelligent. "Not a problem, at all Ms. Velck. We might as well start with the exam of this body, then I'll show you Shelia Voice's body."

They got to work.

* * * *

Meanwhile, Bobby had sent Gabe to interview the witness who had found the body, while he started going over the files of the first victim and studying the pictures Tommy and the team had taken of the second victim. The reporters were hounding him constantly and hovering outside the precinct like vultures. "Stein!" The captain stood behind his desk with a grim look on his face. Bobby sighed and pushed himself up from his desk. He respected the captain a lot, but sometimes he found him to be a pain in his ass. "Hey, Parker, call Nexs and tell him to meet me at the morgue in an hour." He strolled into the captain's office, tapped the door closed behind him, then sauntered over to the desk and rested his butt on the edge of it. "What's up, Cap?"

"Don't give me that smug attitude. I want an update, and I mean now!" Jeremy slammed his fist onto the top of his desk and sat in the chair all the while glaring at Bobby. "Watch your blood pressure Cap. Don't have very much right now, but it seems to be looking like we got a serial killer in the making. First victim was Shelia Voice, aged twenty-five. Worked at a little coffee joint off of Washington Street. Co-workers said she was very pleasant and friendly. Always on time, never causing any trouble, the real honest to goodness girl. Killer bound her wrists and ankles, brutalized her face after burning her eyes out, and deposited the body on the mayor's office steps, which you know already. Killer likes publicity." He started to pace the room. "The second victim is basically the same MO except this time, she was deposited in a well-used park, Dearborn Park. Body was found by an early morning jogger on the east-side of the running trail." Bobby stood gazing out the window while the captain absorbed what he'd said.

Jeremy sat, watching Bobby's back and considering. He was glad he had Stein in his squad. Regardless of what he probably thought, Bobby was his best and he had a lot of faith in him for solving this problem. He only yelled at Bobby because, well, he didn't really know. He did know that Bobby's partner, Gabe, was a lazy shit and if it weren't for Stein, nothing would get solved. "So in other words, you don't have much." Bobby turned from the window and just shrugged his shoulders. "Not much to go on yet. I'm hoping to know more a little later on once Dr. Jackson has had a chance to examine the second body. Then hopefully, I'll be able to give you more. By the way, I've brought Hailey in to help out."

"Christ, Bob! She's a civilian." Jeremy gripped his head. "She knows what she's doing, Cap," he replied. "Get on with it and try to wrap this up quickly but quietly. No leaking things out."

"You know I'd never tell them vultures anything except to go kiss my ass." He opened the door and went back to his desk. Glancing at the clock, he calculated he still had a little more than half an hour before he had to meet Gabe, so he went back to studying the pictures.

*   *   *   *

Six hours of bending over a dead body was not Hailey's way of spending an afternoon, but she did not complain because really, what was the point? Now she was leaning against the big stainless steel sink, drinking a Pepsi and watching Rye finish up with the young woman. In the last few hours, Hailey had decided that Dr. Rye Jackson was a man she could get very used to. He was handsome in a mysterious, nerdy kind of way, very fit, and his voice was the best of all. She had talked to him over the phone, but it was nothing like hearing it in person. It ran over her senses like a good aged whiskey over ice or like sweet ice cream down her throat. She had to force herself not too stare to long at his eyes or she'd lose herself in them. Then there were his work skills. He was very thorough. He examined every inch of the victim's body, not leaving anything out.

He marked everything with appropriate labels and times and cut with such care one would think he was carving the face of the Holy Mother. *His hands.* Hailey couldn't stop watching them. They glided over the body with such compassion and gentleness she couldn't help but wonder how they would feel running over her. Shaking the thoughts out of her head, she stood up, tossed her pop can into the recycle bin and headed back towards the table. Just then, a little Mexican man popped his head in the door and quickly rattled something off to Rye who nodded and waved him away. "What was that all about?" Hailey asked as she glided up beside him. Rye's heart immediately started to hammer away at the sound of her voice so close to his ear, but he cleared his throat and told her that the little man was informing him that a match came back on the victim. He also mentioned that Stein and Nexs would be arriving in about twenty-minute's. Hailey nodded and continued to watch him finish up. Stepping back, he turned and was instantly struck again by her beauty so that all he could do was stare. She stood not two feet, in front of him but all he could do was look into her deep, deep violet eyes and feel himself drift away. In the distance, they heard Bobby's and Gabe's booming voices getting closer but still it didn't register until they heard the swish of the door. They moved apart, but not before Bobby noticed the sexual tension floating around them. Rye broke away first and headed to the sink while Hailey stared down at the body and all of the doctor's notes. "… All I'm saying, Bobby, is that the eyewitness I interviewed was purposefully leaving shit out of his statement." Bobby stood watching Hailey while Gabe rambled on about the witness and how he hated doing grunt work. He walked over to Hailey and leaned up against the autopsy table beside her, and studied her profile. Out of the corner of her eye, Hailey watched him watch her. In all the years that they had been friends, Bobby could always tell when she was unnerved. She turned to him and shot him a look that dared him to speak, but he knew better. He just smiled, turned to face the victim, and called out to Rye, "Find anything new with this one?" Gabe settled back against the wall and motioned for Hailey to join him. Rye finished washing, headed back towards the table, and picked up his notes. Normally, he talked into a recorder, but tonight, he had written everything down because Hailey had been in the room. "Okay. This is basically the same MO as the first victim. Eyes burnt out, chest cavity ripped open, but heart removed with precision. Victim is medium height, light hair. The only difference in each is this one had her tongue cut out, and that is where Hailey found the note. As you know, the first note was located in the small of the back, in a neat incision. Prints came back just before you got here." Rye walked over to the little table beside the door and picked up a white folder. He opened it and walked back to Bobby while reading. "Okay. It says here that this is Marva Lewis, aged twenty-six. I'll have the report typed up, and I'll hand deliver it to you tomorrow morning."

"Great, Doc. We'll talk tomorrow then." Bobby turned and left the room with Gabe following. Hailey hung back and watched as Rye gathered his papers and put away his tools. She walked over to him. "Thank you for letting me examine the bodies, Rye."

"No problem, Hailey. I enjoyed the company." They stood staring at each other then quite suddenly, as if she had just realized what was happening, she turned and left the room, leaving Rye standing there watching after her.

CHAPTER 6

It was 5:00 am. Joyce's alarm clock went off, sending a high, piercing shrill throughout her apartment. She sat up and wondered why she bothered to wake up at all. After dragging herself out of bed, she pulled on her jogging pants and a tank top and headed outside for her morning stretches and jog. Joyce Yuckermin lived on the fifth floor of an old apartment building in the dregs of Seattle. The apartment was cluttered with little knickknacks from all over the place. There was an old, beat-up couch that was more comfortable now than it had ever been and an old re-furnished chair off to the side. A twenty-six-inch television sat in the corner. She had pictures lining her walls, drawings she had done throughout her life and some her mother had sent her. Joyce's kitchen was very small with just enough room for one. The counters were a lime green with black trim around the edges. Her coffee machine sat in the corner with day-old coffee in it, while her fridge lay bare except for a few granny apples, half a jug of milk, and one crusty roll.

Outside, she began her morning stretches then headed off for the park behind her apartment building. Once on the track, her body loosened up and her mind cleared. She thought of nothing else but her feet pounding on the paved path around the park. After five laps, she slowed herself down and started going over her day's schedule: back to the apartment for a quick shower, then to the doctor's office, then grocery shopping. Later on tonight, she would go to work at the little street pub on the corner.

* * * *

Seven in the evening and the door chime tinkled, letting Trevor know someone had entered his pub. Glancing up from his newspaper he saw Joyce heading towards him and he smiled. "Evenin', Joyce! How was it?" She swung the divider up and slipped behind the bar, placing her handbag under the counter while reaching for a mug. "It went well. How about you, Trev?" She poured herself some fresh coffee and smiled at the old man perched on the end stool at the bar.

He graciously tilted his head and raised his glass in to her smile. "Not too bad today. Woke up, and pretty much lounged around till five, then I came down to open up shop. Max there," He pointed down at the old man. "He arrived shortly after I unlocked the door, and now I'm just waiting."

"Guess I'll start cleaning the windows till we get busy." She gathered up the glass cleaner and a rag, then headed over to the windows while Trevor went back to reading his paper.

She had started working for Trevor around three years ago. She had stumbled inside one night and refused to leave till he hired her. It took him till three in the morning to get her out, and ever since then, she'd been working steady and he'd had no complaints. The regulars loved her and the new faces that popped up from time to time fell under her spell as well. Hell, Trevor had to admit he loved having her there. The door tinkled, and in walked Joe Bob. He who was always a very loud man, and this particular night was no different. Joyce, my love, when you gonna marry me?" He bellowed as he scooped her off her chair and swung her around the room like she was a feather. Joe Bob was a bear of a man who stood six feet-seven inches tall and was built like a freight train with scruffy black hair and deep brown eyes. He came to Trev's Place every night without fail. "I'm flattered, Joe Bob, but I could never marry you. I wouldn't want to take your freedom away." He set her down and looked at her with the deepest brown eyes she had seen in a long time. She wondered why she didn't break down. Then, without a thought, he bellowed, "Don't worry, my sweets. I won't let no lady tie me down." His laugh boomed and he headed over to the bar and grabbed a stool. Joyce laughed to herself, shook her head, and turned back to what she was doing.

"How's the construction business, Joe Bob?" Trevor poured his usual, Dark Mountain Ale, and slapped it in front of him. He grinned at Trevor, pulled out a pack of Camels, and snapped his lighter. "Great, man! Got a job over in Norwood village fixin' up some old homes, then got me'self lined up some heavy construction downtown." Joe Bob grabbed his mug and took a big swig. Then he, Max, and Trevor started prattling on about sports and fishing.

Joyce loved working at Trev's Place. She never regretted acting like a fool that first time she walked in. She never meant to grovel, but back then, she was desperate. Three years ago, she had moved to Seattle from Nowheres-ville, Idaho, praying for her life to take her somewhere. For weeks, she searched for work with no luck, and here, she had ended up, Trev's Place. She was cold, hungry, and angry at herself for believing she could do it. She had wandered in and sat down at the end of the bar in the corner and ripped up about a dozen napkins when Trevor slid over to her to say he was closing. That was when her mind snapped and she lost her control. Joyce had glared at him and demanded that he hire her or she wouldn't leave. Trevor had stared at her and burst out laughing. Then he came around the bar, grabbed her arm, and started tugging on her, but she had a firm grip on the end and she just started crying and begging. He didn't have the heart to say no. Ever since then, she'd been happily employed and had an apartment she loved.

Eleven o'clock rolled around, and suddenly, Trev's was off to a steady hum. With Trevor working the bar and Joyce working the floor, everything ran like clockwork, and everyone was having a good time. In the back of the pub, in a dark corner, sat a man drinking a vodka tonic and studying the other patrons with little interest. Then his eyes fell on Joyce, and he straightened in his chair.

He stared intently at her, noting every detail that the naked eye could capture. He watched, as a group of young guys flirted with her and became captivated by her body movements in response to the group. Suddenly, she turned and walked up to the bar, and started talking to Trevor.

"Why must she do that?" He fumbled with his drink and tried to divert his gaze, but he was mesmerized by the way she moved and the jumble of voices in his head kept ranting to him. "Stop it!"

Joyce stood at the bar telling Trevor a story she'd heard from the little old man sitting by the window, when she was tapped on the shoulder. Turning around, she found herself face to face with Billy MacIntyre, who hadn't been in to Trev's Place since last February. "Billy! It's so good to see you!" Joyce said as she smiled and wrapped her arms around him. "It's good to be home and see the gang." He picked her up and swung her while Trevor cracked him a Budweiser and set it down on the bar. Billy MacIntyre was twenty-eight and had been a bona fide stock-car racer since he was old enough to drive. The previous year, he'd gone on a tour and won the championship stock-car race. He had been traveling ever since. This was the first time he had been home since he left over a year ago. "How was the travel, Billy?" Trevor asked, while pouring more and more beers. He slid half down the bar to pass the some to Joyce. "Real good Trevor, Went to Europe, Ireland, and even stopped over in Africa for a couple nights. Saw some really excellent, things man." Billy sat back on the bar stool chair and waved at Joe Bob who was arguing loudly with Max about the football game last night. The flow of customers was still going strong, and Courtney, the other waitress, was late again. The house band, 'Origin', was just setting up for their twelve o'clock show. Nobody noticed the tall, attractive man wearing a long dark coat exit quietly out the door.

*   *   *   *

Back at the precinct, Bobby, Gabe, Hailey and Rye were all seated around the squad "thinking" table, as everyone liked to call it. On a cork-board, many pictures taken from different angles were pinned up of the two victims, and little notes were attached on a few of them. The two notes the killer left were also among the pictures. Hailey was studying one of the photos of the first victim, Shelia Voice, while Bobby and Rye conversed over an open file. Gabe straddled a chair and listened to their conversation. "What are these markings here?" Hailey turned from the photograph she was studying and looked at the trio sitting at the table. Bobby stood up and walked over to the photo. He stared intently at the spot she pointed out. "I don't see nothin'." He squinted some more. "It's right there. Slightly behind her ear and under the lobe, see it? It kind of looks like an ink smudge." Rye was shuffling through some photos on the table and found the one they were looking at. He grabbed his magnifying glass. "I never noticed it during the examination, and I've only done the post. It could be a birthmark, or maybe a tattoo of some sort. No … wait. She had no distinguishing markings. I don't know what it is." Hailey contemplated the mark. Her gut was trying to tell her something, and she had learn-t to listen to it, so all she said was, "Maybe." She turned away from the cork board and sat down at the table across from Rye, beside Bobby. Rye's and Hailey's eyes briefly met, and in that instant, heat flared between them. Gabe was oblivious to it. Bobby settled back into his seat and pulled out a stick of gum. "We need to establish motive. So far, all I can think of is the perp is fucking whacked out." Hailey watched Bobby and realized that he was extremely ragged, like he hadn't slept in days, and then it dawned on her that he probably hadn't. At most, he'd probably only had two hours of sleep in two days, which wouldn't surprise her at all. She felt concerned about him and promised herself she would cook him some dinner tonight. "I'm not an expert on psychotic behavior, but I feel that the perpetrator is in pain, and he doesn't enjoy the things he does, but feels it's for the good of the victim … what's best. That is why, I believe, he burns the eyes to prevent the victim from showing him the pain he causes them, and he keeps the heart, not for a prize, but to remember the girl," Rye stated with the hesitancy of one not used to talking in big groups. Hailey studied him from her chair. She noticed the little twitch start, just above his eyebrow, when he started talking. She found it oddly adorable. She loved the way his eyes lit up when he said something. They were full of self-assuredness and passion. She glided from one person to the next, taking in their moods, which was second nature to her now. Gabe was off in his own world, not really there but listening, while Bobby was still contemplating what Rye had said and evidently concentrating very hard because he had his eyes scrunched up. "I have to agree with some of what you said. I feel he does think he's delivering help to his victims and that he hates what he's doing. At the same time, though, he feels very powerful and he takes the heart because of this feeling. The burning of the eyes signifies his fear of secrets. What he is doing and his identity must remain passive, lifeless. I feel he doesn't want to be caught but knows that he must." Hailey sat back, and Bobby looked at her. "How in the hell do you figure that?" She smiled, shrugged her shoulders, and said, "I know a few things about deranged people. I was trained to spot them." She left it at that. Bobby scowled at her. "One of these days, you're going to tell me about your navy days, damn it!" Rye's brows went up in surprise at the comment, and Gabe leaned over and whispered in his ear, "Bobby's been tryin' to get it out of her for years."

"She was in the navy?" Rye whispered back. "For how long?" Gabe just smiled and shrugged his shoulders. Bobby stood up and paced the room, hoping to release his frustration and to mull over Hailey's analysis of the killer. "Okay. We all agree that the killer is fucked up. The victims both have blond hair and the same build. The wounds are identical except for Marva Lewis and her missing tongue. Each victim had a note and was left in a populated places. No prints anywhere. Fuck! We have bare minimum to go on, and it's making me crazy!" Bobby slammed his fist into the wall and let out a string of curses when his hand started to throb. "What about the old case you were lookin' through?" Gabe piped up. "Find anything useful?" Bobby stopped and glanced at Gabe. "They're not the same. Too many little differences."

"What about the notes?" Gabe asked. "What's the perp tryin' to say?" Hailey turned to Gabe with an amused look and waited for Bobby to say something. He stopped pacing. "That's a good question. I think we should ask Hailey." All three of them looked at her and waited. Huffing, she rolled her eyes and stood up. "All right. I've been slowly thinking them over. I can say that the perp is probably very well educated, maybe Catholic, and we can expect more of them." She stood at the board with her back to the guys and thought, *I just need a little more time, guys. Then I'll answer the rest.* "That's it?" Bobby demanded. "I thought you were trained in analyzing psychos." He sneered at her. She turned around and glared, "Fuck you Bobby." It was said with quiet calm but her eyes screamed murder, and she turned and left the room. "Shit!" he roared and slammed his hand on the table. "Smooth, Bobby. Real smooth." Gabe chuckled to himself and stretched his arms behind his head while winking at Rye who sat dumbfounded.

*   *   *   *

"Hello all!" Courtney greeted the bar as she strolled in a half-hour late. "Courtney. You're late … again. Third time this week." Trevor spoke with a relaxed tone and eyed her out of the corner of his eye, all the while remaining in stride with the flow of beer and drinks. Courtney grinned, she was used to this, and fluttered her lashes at him. "I know, Trevor, and I'm sorry, but it couldn't be helped." She lifted the divider, donned her apron, and grabbed her tray. "Nice of you to make it, Court. I hope it wasn't a bother for you to be here?" Joyce asked, not expecting a reply. She quickly gave her a run-down then slipped behind the bar and began to help Trevor. "Damn girl," he muttered and grinned. "Gotta love her!" Joe Bob's voice boomed out, drowning out the crowd for a few seconds while Courtney sashayed her way around the bar.

*   *   *   *

Across the street, he waited in the shadows. "Ab uno disce omnes", **(from one specimen judge of all the rest.)** *He wrestled with the hate throbbing inside him. She infuriated him but also made him want. He hated wanting. The voices were louder than before. Each day was a struggle with sanity, and he blamed his parents. They were the ones who forced him into this life he led. He was trained to show nothing, but in time, two different people emerged, unbeknownst to Mommy and Daddy. What he had become, they taught him to be: the ever-successful, witty, and charming businessman, and then there was this. This feeling right now in the dark recesses of his mind drove him to insanity. He hated their remedy, but it was the only thing to quiet the voices. Hidden in the shadows, he waited for her. The big, loud man had called her Joyce. He ranted to himself in Latin. He closed his eyes for a moment. What did he just say? "Aut vincere aut mori, cum privilegio." He knew Latin from his Catholic days and now struggled with the translation,* **"Either to conquer or to die; death or victory, with privilege."** *He smiled to himself. That night, he would meet her for the first and final time.*

CHAPTER 7

It was eight in the morning. Rye stood in front of his office window looking out over the staff parking lot. A sleek, dark metallic blue Mustang pulled into the lot and parked in Dr. Jacobson's spot. He admired the car and noticed that it was a '65 Mustang. He was stunned when he saw Hailey step out of the car and quickly closed his mouth, less she notice him standing there. I shouldn't be surprised, he thought. He watched as Hailey stroked the car with tenderness and grinned to himself. She probably built it herself.

Hailey knew he was watching. She had seen his look of stunned disbelief when she had gotten out of the car. She could feel his eyes on her. She didn't care, though. She was too in awe of herself to care if she looked a little loony stroking her car. Her own sweat, blood, and curses went into it, and she was damn proud. Hailey glanced quickly over her shoulder and noticed his grin. Gathering herself, she headed for the building and Rye's office. They had a lot of work to do, and she preferred to get started now.

"Good morning, Hailey." Rye smiled at her and handed her a mug of fresh, hot, and strong black coffee. Smiling back, she accepted the coffee and inhaled deeply. "Thanks and good morning to you, Doc." Rye nodded and motioned to the high-back chair in front of the desk. She sat and took in the room. His office was tucked on the third floor in the west corner. His desk took up a small portion of the room while the rest was filled with file cabinets and shelves covered in binders and books. There were files stacked on the two corners of his desk and more on the floor beside it. His diplomas were tacked on the walls to her left, and on the right was a picture of a sunset over the sea. He settled himself in his chair, pulled the two case files on the victims out from one of the piles, and placed them in front of her. "What, exactly, are we looking for?"

"Every killer leaves something behind, even the most careful. I plan on finding the clue he left us, and you're going to help me. One very important lesson I learned during my time was that death always has a story to tell." Hailey reached over, took a file, and opened it. "We're the ones who are going to stop this killer, and we had better move quickly. I'm pretty sure this guy is going to kill again and soon."

"First off, how do you know it's a man, and second, what time?" He sat there studying her and realized he couldn't read her at all. "I just know. This is an act of hate, but the killer has compassion." She ignored his second question and continued to read the file. "Ray is pulling the two victims out for us. I still have to do the post exam, but I'll let you check out the bodies first." He stood and headed for the autopsy suite with Hailey right behind him.

Sheila Voice's body lay on the cold, steel table in the center of the room. Off to the right, against the wall, were metal carts neatly lined with instruments, test tubes, boxes of latex gloves, and various sized covered scalpels. Across the room stood a deep metal sink and counter. Above the counter were cubbyholes filled with camera equipment and film. Hailey stood beside the table looking down at Shelia Voice. She knew that Shelia had once been a very pretty woman who had a life to live, but it was cut short by a mad-man. Rye handed Hailey a pair of gloves, and she started to examine the body. Lifting the right arm, she noticed a dark spot just below the armpit. It was about the size of a quarter but elongated. "This mark isn't in any of the pictures." Rye came over to the table and studied the mark she was pointing out. "It wasn't there when I examined her earlier. I'm not sure what it's from." Hailey nodded and continued on. "Let's dig in." Rye grinned at her and wheeled a cart over. "Sorry, morbid humor." Hailey smiled and stepped back so he could get in. "Could you take notes for me? I usually record, but it's easier to write when there're people around." He handed her a clipboard. Using a small, thin scalpel, he slowly made an incision at the base of the throat, moving up and under the chin. He then made two lateral cuts at the base of the first cut and peeled the skin away. She drew the incision and quickly wrote what he said. The chest was ripped open so Rye just had to remove the organs. He started with the lungs and placed them gently in Hailey's hands, and she weighed them then placed them in a plastic dish. Then came the liver, kidneys, and the intestines which each were weighed and placed in appropriate dishes. The flower Rye had earlier found in place of the heart was removed from refrigeration and placed among the rest of the organs. They then gathered the proper vials and collected fluid from the body. Rye motioned to Hailey to bring the lungs over to the counter where there were microscopes in various sizes lined against the wall. He carefully cut into the left lung and removed some of the inner tissue and placed it in a petri dish. He then put the dish under the fourth scope lined against the wall. While he was leaning over, she toured the room with her eyes. He grunted and motioned for her to look.

"Interesting, isn't it? Do you see the light dusting of the tissue?" She nodded and straightened. "What is it?"

"I'm not sure. It could be she inhaled something right before he took her." Rye removed the dish, capped and labeled it, and placed it on a shelf in the mini fridge on the counter. Hailey's mind was reeling with possibilities. "Do you mind if I take a sample? I have a friend I'd like to have take a look." He watched her and couldn't help but wonder if her friend was more than a friend. "Sure, I don't see why not." She placed some in a dish and pocketed it. Rye examined the other organs, Hailey jotted notes down on the clipboard. They then went over the next body.

Marva Lewis lay on another cold steel table beside Sheila. Examining the body, Hailey found two marks similar to the ones on Sheila Voice's body. When she was finished, Rye, again, made the same incisions and removed the same organs while Hailey documented and weighed everything. "Nothing was left in place of the heart, and the tongue is missing," Hailey said to the air. He nodded and collected a sample of the right lung tissue and placed it under the same scope he'd used before. "Got the same light dusting here so both ladies inhaled something before they died. Tests will tell us what it is, and I'll be sure to put a rush on them. They're kinda slow in the labs." They cleaned up the bodies, put everything away, and went up to Rye's office. Once they were settled, Ray, the little Mexican man Hailey had glimpsed before, was standing at the door, and Rye sent him off to the labs with the samples and made sure he understood that they were to rush the results. Hailey's cell phone buzzed in her pocket, making her flinch. It was Bobby. He and Gabe were on their way over.

*   *   *   *

"Ace to Rover ..."

"Rover here. In-coming, nine o'clock, looks like spades with toys. Gather them up, over." *Explosions rock the ground. Dust and debris cloak the squad. Running for cover, Jones, Patrick, and Gunns are taken out ... She hits the ground firing and fades out ...*

Jolting awake, drenched in sweat, Hailey rolled out of bed, crouched, and reached for her weapon that didn't exist. Groggy and unfocused, she slowly stood up and rubbed her face, taking deep, calming breaths to steady her heart. She hadn't had that dream for a few months now, and it had shaken her. She had almost lost her life in that memory, and she had lost most of her friends. Standing over the sink with the cold water running, Hailey stared at her reflection while images flashed through her mind. Dipping her hand under the flow, she closed her eyes and splashed water on her face.

Down in the kitchen, she started water for tea and realized that she was up for the day even though it was only 3:30 in the morning. She'd have her tea and go for her jog, but she would add a couple of miles. Sitting down at the kitchen table, Hailey gazed out the deck door and thought of nothing but her tea. Prepping her mind for the jog was a ritual with her. Her sergeant in the Marines had taught her that total focus helped heighten the two major senses. Finishing her tea, she stood, grabbed her key, and headed out the door.

*   *   *   *

Bobby was still in bed at four in the morning, but he wasn't asleep. Lying on his back, he stared up at the ceiling with his mind running full force with questions and scenarios. Where did the killer snag them? Had he met them before he killed them? Why did he take the heart and why the tongue? It was driving him mad. It was all chaotic. He threw the covers off, stomped into the kitchen, and flicked on the coffee. Nobody else liked his coffee so he was forbidden to make coffee at the precinct, but he found nothing wrong with it. It was perfect coffee in his mind. He went into his office and booted up his computer. He spread some pictures out. Something was nagging him about the cases; he just had to find it. After grabbing some coffee, he sat down at the desk and scanned the files again looking for God knows what, but something. His eyes roamed over the pictures. Suddenly, his gut tightened. He quickly picked up the photograph of the first victim's chest cavity. Bobby sifted through the drawer and pulled out his magnifying glass, focusing on the arteries connecting the heart. There was some white substance on the edges of the incision. He clicked on her autopsy report and scanned it for any mention of the residue. Finding none, he reached for the phone, then, remembering that it was only four thirty or five in the morning, let his hand fall. Fuck it, he thought. I'll wake Gabe up. Gabe picked up on the fourth ring. "Huh?" he grunted into the receiver. "Morning, Gabe!" Bobby yelled joyfully. "Waddaya want?" He could hear sheets rustle and springs squeak as he pictured Gabe standing up. "Couldn't sleep and was going over the files again. Get your ass outta bed and come over." Gabe yawned, grunted, and hung-up. Bobby placed the receiver back and relaxed against the chair feeling much better now. Half an hour later, he heard Gabe pull up in the driveway and went to unlock the door. Pouring his third mug of coffee and pulling out a mug for Gabe, he heard him cursing away at everything and especially Bobby. He grinned and strutted out of the kitchen, handing Gabe his coffee. They headed to his office. "What the hell, Bobby? What's so damn important that I had to drag myself over here?"

"I needed to show someone this." He slid the picture of Sheila's chest cavity over to Gabe and passed him the magnifying glass. "What do you notice about that picture?" Gabe hunched over it and slowly examined the picture. Bobby knew the instant Gabe noticed the powder. "Well, holy shit! What is it?"

"I have no idea, but it's not in any of the autopsy reports. Each victim seems to have that white powder in the same places. The only mention of a white powder substance is in the victim's lungs, suggesting inhalation." Bobby shuffled through some papers. He found what he needed and handed it to Gabe. He skimmed over the information. "It doesn't say what it is."

"I know. Rye is running tests still. He should have the results by mid-afternoon. He put an extreme rush on them. What I want to know though, is if the women inhaled something, why is there some by the incisions?" Gabe frowned. "What if it isn't even the same substance?" They both went silent, caught up in their thoughts. "I'll call Hailey in about an hour or so and get her take on it."

*   *   *   *

Having showered and dressed after her run, Hailey settled down in her desk chair and picked up the phone. Glancing at the clock, she noticed it was eight in the morning. Her run had lasted longer than she had intended. "Ramsey here." With the phone cradled on her shoulder, she heard that familiar deep rumbling flow out from the ear-piece; she grinned. "Good to hear that voice, Kage! How the hell have you been?"

"Hailey! Is that you I'm hearing?" Ramsey Kage was Hailey's second in command in her unit during their time. He hadn't heard from her in a few years, but he had kept tabs on her. He was glad to hear from her, but he wondered what she needed from him and how long it would take for her to ask. He knew she hated asking for any kind of help. "So how's the PI business treating ya?" She leaned back in her chair with a smile. "It's treating me fairly. How's the Fed business? Catch any bad guys lately?"

"Actually, I'm working on a humdinger of one now. Let's cut the crap, Lieutenant. What can I help you with? Cause Lord knows I owe you." He sat back and waited for her to respond. Her grin faded as the memory came crashing back. Clearing her throat, she told him about the case she was helping out with. "I have a few ideas in mind about the killer, but I was hoping, if you have some time, you could do up a profile for me." He sat quietly, lost in his thoughts. The case he was profiling now was similar to what she was talking about but he wondered how that could be possible when his case was situated in Oakland. Maybe there was a team ripping hell up, or maybe the world just had two new psycho's running loose. "I'll see what I can do." Next, Hailey booted up her computer and opened the file she had created on the perpetrator and reread her notes. She was missing something, but she couldn't pin point it. She was determined she would. As she picked up her mug of tea, the phone rang, jarring her. She grabbed the receiver. "Velck Private Investigations."

"It's Bobby. Whatcha doin'?"

"Working. How about you?" Hailey took a sip of her tea and waited.

"How about that! Gabe and myself are doing the same thing. Why don't you come on over to the house and we can all work together?"

"I have a better idea, Bobby. Why don't the two of you come over here and we can work in my office?"

They were over in fifteen minutes.

CHAPTER 8

She was still sitting behind her desk scouring her files when Bobby strutted in with Gabe sauntering behind him. Gabe dropped the files he'd brought over on the edge of her desk and grabbed a chair in the corner to have a cigar. Hailey looked at him and with a flick of her wrist, sent him out to the deck. He grumbled something and went out the door. Bobby laughed and pulled a chair up beside her. "Found something in the autopsy pictures. Check it out. You'll need this." He handed her the picture and his magnifying glass. "Look around the arteries. Do you see anything?" She noticed it immediately. A white substance was dusted around the incisions. "It's not in the autopsy files, right?" She looked up and read his answer in his face. "Could be from gloves the killer used or maybe even the staff at the medical examiner's office." He sat there and contemplated that tidbit. He hadn't even thought of that. "I don't think any of Rye's team is that careless, but I'll call him and check it out." He picked up Hailey's phone and dialed. A quiet male voice answered. Bobby identified himself and asked to speak with Dr. Jackson. The quiet voice informed him that Dr. Jackson was in the middle of an examination and asked if it was urgent. He said yes so the voice placed him on hold. Classical music flowed into his ear, and he groaned inwardly. Hailey was back to scanning her notes and adding more about the white substance.

"Dr. Jackson here. What's up Detective?"

"Found something you should look into. Musta missed it during your examination of the bodies. A white substance around the arteries in the victim pictures. It wasn't in the autopsy reports. Only that stuff you found in the lungs. Maybe it's the same thing. Did your labs find any matches yet?"

"I haven't checked, but I'll send my assistant there now. I can't remember any white substance around that area of the chest cavity, but I'll definitely take a look. These cases keep getting weirder by the minute."

"Yes they do. How about those spots Hailey found. Any word on those?"

"Yup. Got the report right here. They're bruises caused from a metal object clamped on the skin. It had to have been a type of restraint. Maybe used when

38

he burnt out their eyes. Found traces of iron in the skin around those areas." *Clamps. Why would he use metal clamps?* Bobby couldn't think about the possibilities right now; he'd worry about that aspect later. "Thanks, Rye. I'll get a hold of you later." He hung up. Turning to Hailey, he scanned what she was reading. *Flour?* "What the hell are you reading?" She ignored him and scrolled down the page. Bobby tapped her shoulder. Glancing at him, she lifted her brow. He stared at her. "I'm reading up on white substances … why?" She turned and faced him, waiting for a response. "Flour? How could that have anything to do with the cases?" he huffed in authorization and leaned back in his chair. Hailey just shook her head. "You can kill a person with pretty much anything." Bobby sat there. How could she always do that to him? He had to remind himself that she used to be in the Marines, a SEAL to be exact. She'd probably seen worse than he ever had in his entire police career. He just accepted her words and nodded. "Okay, but you should look up clamps made of iron." Hailey faced the computer again, and her fingers flew across the keyboard. Gabe stumbled back in and dragged a chair into the circle around her desk. "Holy shit, girl! You got quicksilver fingers!" He grinned at her. Hailey didn't even break stride while she smiled up at him. Catching a flash of the word *iron*, she suddenly stopped typing and flexed her fingers. She asked Bobby exactly why she was looking this up, and he told her it was about the spots she'd found. "Turns out they were bruises and were made by a clamp of some sort made of iron." Images of all shapes, styles, and sizes of clamps flashed through her mind while her hand worked the mouse scrolling down the screen. Her mind settled on one before she scrolled to it. She took a sharp intake of breath.

* * * *

Rye was sitting at his desk when Ray walked in with the report from the lab. "Those lab guys are a real bunch of cards, Doc. They said to tell you that they aren't finished but to give you what they do have." He tossed it on the desk and left the office. Stretching his sore muscles, Rye picked up the report and slowly read through it. There was nothing found in any of the organs except the lungs. The stomach was empty so he concluded that Shelia Voice had not eaten prior to her death and the same with Marva Lewis. Marva did have a kidney infection, but besides the prescription drugs in her system, nothing else was found. The lab still had to distinguish the substance found in the lungs.

Sighing, he stood and gazed out his window. The sun was bright today, and he wished he were on the water sailing. He picked up his coffee mug and took a sip. Noticing that it was empty, he went to the lunch-room and got a third cup. The coffee was stronger than usual, meaning it had been on for awhile now, but he didn't care. Strong coffee was better than no coffee. Walking back to his office, Rye stopped and peeked inside Sara Wilmson's office. She was hunched over her microscope with a pen in her left hand and a mug of steaming tea in the other. He watched her for a couple of seconds then strolled over to stand beside her. He tapped her shoulder, and she jerked back almost dumping her tea on him. "Son of a bitch, Rye! Don't sneak up on me like that. How long have you been there?" She squinted at him through horn-rimmed glasses and waited for a reply. He studied her face. She had very clear hazel eyes that shouted every emotion. Her face was slender with a short-button shaped nose and bow-tie lips a pale rose in color. Short cropped black hair stood up everywhere on her small head and her lab coat fluttered around her small, shapely body. Rye had no doubt she ran every day and probably lifted a few weights now and again. Clearing his throat, he shuffled his feet "Sorry, Sara. I've been standing here about five minutes. What are you looking at?" He gestured towards the microscope and stepped up to take a look when she stepped back. "It's a piece of liver. One of my cases had the most advanced case of liver disease I've ever seen, and I wanted to get a closer look at it." Rye took a peek and inhaled sharply at the sight. It was, in short, disgusting. It looked like a shriveled-up raisin with a bit of slimy residue covering it. He straightened up and shook his head. How anyone could let their organs get so bad was a mystery to him. "I'm assuming that was the cause of death?"

"Actually no. Someone knifed him in the back right between the shoulder blades. If that hadn't gotten him, though, he would've died very soon from that liver." Sara stretched and removed the slide, then filed it away. "Is there something you wanted?" He shrugged and leaned against her desk. "I've got a couple of weird cases going on. Working with Detectives Stein and Nexs and a PI they brought in on it. We found some bruises on the bodies, but the weird thing is that they didn't show up till after the bodies were admitted. Thought maybe you could take a look." Sara sighed inwardly. She was hoping Rye would ask her out, but that did not seem to be the focus of his thoughts. She stood up. "Sure, I'll take a look. Have you established the cause of the bruises?"

"The lab found traces of iron around the marks. Said they were probably caused by some sort of clamp. Plus, I found a white residue in the lungs, and the lab still hasn't been able to find out its origin. They're slagging it down there lately." They walked down the stairs side by side and entered the autopsy suite. Rye pulled on a pair of surgical gloves and walked over to the body fridge. He wheeled out Shelia Voice's body, and Sara started examining the bruises. "Interesting." Rye stood beside her. His thoughts had drifted for a moment, but he focused on the body in front of him. "It's pretty harsh. Look at the eyes, or rather the sockets. The killer burnt out the eyes first … then ripped the chest open, brutally. He does have skills, though. Look how clean the cuts are around where the heart was removed. Very clean, very precise. The face was beaten after death." Rye leaned in closer to the chest cavity. There, by the ventricles, was the white substance Bobby had mentioned. It was no wonder he had missed it before, it was hardly noticeable. He scraped some into a petri dish. He'd personally take it down to the lab and wait there while they tested it. "If the beatings were done after death, why, do you think, did he bother?" Sara asked, almost to herself it seemed, as she leaned closer towards the face. "The sooner this guy is caught, the better we'll all feel." She glanced at Rye, and her heart did a little flutter. Sighing, she turned and started to clean up. "Rye, I'm not sure what could have caused those marks, possibly a clamp but truthfully, I kinda doubt that's what caused them. I mean, why would he clamp them? I'll study them tonight and get back to you." She gathered her samples and went back to her office. He cleaned up once again and placed the body back in the fridge. He grabbed his samples and headed for the labs.

*   *   *   *

Hailey was still sitting in front of her computer four hours later. Bobby and Gabe had gone back to the precinct to follow up on some leads that had been called in. Hailey had no doubt that those leads would be dead ends. After shutting down her computer, she locked up her office and headed out. She had an idea, and she hoped it panned out.

Outside a seedy little strip joint in the dregs of downtown Seattle, she locked up her car, went inside, and grabbed a seat at the bar. The bartender sent her a quizzical look but sauntered up to her to take her order. Slowly, she scanned the room. A lot of under agers and some lowlifes were occupying the pool tables at the far end, but a further scan revealed that her informant wasn't present. Turning back towards the bar, she took a sip of her tonic water and decided to wait him out. She knew Scrum would eventually show up. After all, it was only about seven in the evening and he couldn't go more than a few hours without coming here. The strippers all knew him by name, and, believe it or not, they treated him kindly. Scrum was by far the ugliest guy around, but anyone who knew him knew that he was only that way because of a house fire he got caught in as a child. After a drunken quarrel with his mother, his father had set the house ablaze when she and the boy had gone to bed. Hailey only used Scrum for information when the cases involved deranged people, and, in her mind, this killer was extremely deranged. She didn't even know what Scrum's real name was, and, if she was honest with herself, she didn't want to know.

She didn't even care how he knew what he knew. The bar door opened, filling the place with light and fresh air for the briefest of moments. Glancing over her shoulder, she caught a glimpse of jeans, a tee shirt, and scraggly black hair. She smiled to herself and slowly turned around. Scrum's beady little eyes made contact, and he gave a little nod towards the back of the room where no one was seated. She grabbed her drink, ordered a Bud for him, and walked over to where he had seated himself. "Hey, Scrum. How's it hanging?" She pulled out a chair and settled herself so that she could see the rest of the bar. The lowlifes were trying to pick a fight with the under agers but weren't succeeding. Scrum was chugging his beer back, and after a loud smacking sound, he wiped his mouth on his sleeve. "Not too bad, Miss PI. Did you catch the game last night? It was a good one."

"Listen, Scrum … I need a favor if you can manage it." Scrum glanced up from the table. His eyes sparkled, and a grin slid across his face. "Favor? Where's the green?" She chuckled softly. "How long have we known each other, Scrum? Two years, isn't it? The green is always a friend." Scrum shrugged as if he didn't care. "What's the favor, Miss PI?" After pulling out a dark envelope from her pocket, she slid it across the table. He stared at it but didn't reach for it. He knew enough to wait. Beside the envelope, she placed a small pile of paper, which she gestured to Scrum to take. "I need you to find me that specific type of clamp … and fast." His beady eyes studied the picture while Hailey made a phone call on her cell. Quietly, she briefly explained the favor to Bobby. He didn't reply, so she hung up.

"How about it, Scrum? Can you manage it?" He nodded, stuffed the envelope in his pocket, and left the papers on the table. "I'll be in touch, Miss PI."

CHAPTER 9

"Stop!" Gabe yelled at the tall, slender Mexican running away from him. He tackled him from behind, and they both fell in a heap on the sidewalk. "*Why the hell did you run, Sancho?*" The Mexican mumbled something into the cement, Gabe hauled him up and started dragging him towards the car. "I just have some questions for you, and you *will* answer them, right, Sancho?" He nodded, and Gabe all but threw him in the back seat of the car. "How have you been? Staying out of trouble?" Sancho simply nodded and avoided the detective's eyes. He wished he'd never run into Detective Nexs. He needed a fix and bad. He knew he shouldn't have run, but it was like his body just took over and darted. He had been running from cops since he was six and his older brother was leader of the 'Guerra al Cuchillo,' which in English translated to "War to the Knife." His brother had been dead now for ten years, knifed in the back during his time in the pen. Sancho vowed never to get stuck in that pit, so occasionally, he helped out Nexs. The rest of the time, he avoided him.

Gabe was studying Sancho. He noticed the glaze in his eyes and cursed softly. It looked like he was still into the drugs, which Gabe felt slightly responsible for. About three years back, Nexs had arrested Sancho for prostitution and drugs. He was only eighteen at that time, and Gabe had made a deal with him. Sancho gave up the leader of the prostitution ring and served community hours for the drug charge. Since then, he'd been his snitch, whenever he could find him. "Heard of the killings, Sancho?" Sancho nodded grimly and glanced up at him. "I read about' em. Why?"

"Have any idea about who mighta done it?"

"No way, man! I don't know nothin', and I didn't see nothin'!" He crossed his arms over his chest and slouched lower in the seat. "You're not telling me something, Sancho. What is it?" He squirmed in the seat. "I don't know nothin', man. Leave me alone."

"You're lying." Gabe tossed his cigar out the window, his gaze intent on Sancho's head, since he was staring at his lap. Suddenly, he looked up, straight into Gabe's eyes. "The first victim ... what was her name?"

"Her name? It was Shelia Voice. Did you know her, Sancho?" He groaned and clutched his stomach like he was dying. "I knew her, yes. She worked for me." Gabe was startled. Worked for him? Doing what? he wondered. "What do you mean, 'worked for' you?" Sancho grimaced. "She was one of my girls, Detective, one of my favorites. She was most beautiful, with her blond hair and pale blue eyes. She was good at her work too, but it was only a hobby for her. She worked during the day at some little coffee joint." Gabe was stunned. "She's not beautiful anymore, Sancho. When was the last time you saw her?"

"I saw her last Friday. I sent her to a regular who specifically asked for her." Gabe's temper was beginning to flare, and Sancho knew it. Quickly, he stuttered out, "Understand that my girls have a right to sleep with or not sleep with, the john's who take them out. My business is clean." Gabe didn't care. His eyes sent out lethal vibes, which seemed to singe Sancho. "How many girls you got, Sancho?"

"Only five girls now, now that my Shelia is gone. Can I go now?" Gabe rolled down his window and quietly spoke to him. "Don't go too far, Sancho. I'll be back to talk to you." He started up the car and drove away with Sancho staring after.

Back at his desk, Gabe was still fuming. "Nexs! How's it hanging, man?" Charlie Makrow stood next to Gabe and poured himself a cup of the brew. Charlie had been with the force for twenty-five years, and Gabe held little respect for him. He was the head dispatcher and quite the asshole, in Gabe's mind. "Fine Charlie. You?" Charlie smiled, showing very crooked teeth, and nodded vigorously. "Fine, fine. How's that case coming along? Quite a grue-some one, isn't it?" He nodded and walked back to his desk scowling. Sancho knew something, and he'd be damned if he didn't pry it out of him. Bobby came out of the captain's office and headed for his desk. "Find out anything? Grab your coat, and fill me in on the way. We're off to Hailey's."

* * * *

After returning from her talk with Scrum, Hailey settled back in front of her computer and continued her search for the toxin found in the victims. *It's like finding a needle in a haystack,* she thought. *What I need are the components of the chemical compound, and then I can narrow down the search.* She picked up the phone and dialed Rye's office. "ME's office." Hailey asked to be connected to Dr. Jackson. While she sat listening to the elevator music, she continued to scan the screen. "Dr Jackson."

"Rye, Hailey here. Just curious as to the test results on that substance you found?"

"Hailey. I'm afraid the lab hasn't found anything useful yet."

"Have they figured out the compound's components yet?"

"Ummm … not sure. I'll find out. Call you back." She hung up the phone. Maybe it was nothing. Maybe the powder was nothing more than talcum powder from some careless assistant's gloves, left when they were moving the body into the fridge perhaps. If that was the case, then how come the lab hadn't gotten a hit? *Because they haven't even tested it yet.* Hailey got up and strode to the window. *Fucking lab techs! Doesn't this case have priority?* Sighing, she ran her hand through her hair and went back to the computer. As she was booting it up, Gabe and Bobby walked in. "Hey. What's the scowl for?" Flopping himself into a chair, Bobby popped a candy in his mouth, crossed his hands, and watched Hailey scowl at the computer. "Just thinking about that powder. It has no relevance to the murders, and we need to focus on the bruises."

"If the powder is nothing more than talcum, why haven't the lab techs figured that out?" Both turned and stared at Gabe. Hailey shrugged her shoulders and turned to the computer. The phone rang. "Velck Investigations."

"Hailey. I think I might have found something for you." She sat facing the screen with the phone cradled between her neck and shoulder. "Ramsey. How are you?" Bobby and Gabe headed onto the porch to have a smoke but Bobby made sure to leave the door open a crack to listen to her side of the conversation. "Who's Ramsey?" Gabe asked Bobby. He shrugged his shoulders and looked out across the lake towards the setting sun and tuning his ears to Hailey's voice.

"What have you found, Ramsey? Please tell me something good."

"I put together that profile you wanted. It's a little thin, but I think it'll help."

"Anything you can manage will help."

"I'm sending it to a private file labeled 'KROSS,' access number 6229. About the other thing you asked me to look into, I couldn't find anything." Hailey clicked her mouse and opened her e-mail selecting "Profile22698-KROSS" and typed the access number. "Thanks, Ramsey. I'll talk to you later then." She hung up the phone and skimmed through the file.

Subject 5587. Case file KROSS. Based on available amount of evidence, subject seems to have a deep case of schizophrenia. Deep emotional roots leading to subject at hand. Probable cause: home life as a child was abusive or witness to violent death. Mutilation of victims represents symbolic meaning on a morbid level. Burning of eyes may symbolize a secret, one he is keeping, and the missing heart could be symbolic of lost love or a longing for love. Bodies left in public areas and notes left behind are showing that the subject wants to be stopped and understands on a basic level that what subject is doing is wrong. Further analysis pending. Subject will keep killing till caught. End of file. Subject 5587.

She sat back in her chair and let out a breath. Schizophrenia didn't mesh right. Maybe it was not full schizophrenia, perhaps a light case, if that was even possible. Bobby came back inside with Gabe in tow. "Anything interesting on the phone?" He watched her closely. He could almost see the gears churning in that mind of hers. Shaking her head, she brought herself out of her thoughts and focused on Bobby. "What did you ask me?" She smiled. "I asked if that phone call was helpful." Gabe watched from the corner of the room. "Who's Ramsey?"

"Who? Oh, Ramsey. He's a profiler for the FBI. I asked him to do up a profile on the killer. It's there on the screen if you want to read it. Actually, I'll print it out." She hit a few keys, and the printer spit out a sheet. Bobby picked it up and read it over. Hailey got up, fixed herself some tea, and went to stand in front of the deck doors. The lake was calm and smooth, and the sun was setting, giving the lake a golden shimmer that looked like gold dust settling. She glanced at her watch. Bobby set the paper down. "That's a pretty basic profile but helpful, I think. I've had a few inspirations. Gabe and I are going to go check a few things, and we'll hook up tomorrow, say noon at the precinct?" She nodded, and Gabe gathered his jacket. "Till tomorrow then." They went out the office deck doors, and Hailey locked up and went upstairs.

CHAPTER 10

Surrounded by darkness, Joyce huddled on the floor hugging her knees. She wasn't sure how long she'd been sitting there in this same spot where she had woken up. She had tried screaming for help but gave up. Now she sat silently with tears rolling down her cheeks, trying to figure out how she got to wherever the hell she was. The last thing she remembered was rounding the corner from the bar and hearing a strange whispering behind her. She didn't dare turn around, fearful of what she might find. She had a deep gut feeling that wherever she was, it was her death-bed.

Upstairs, he sat in the beam of one lamp, sunk into his favorite chair. The voices ran rampant through his head. He tossed his last sip of brandy down his throat and threw the glass against the wall where it shattered. He grabbed his head and shook it back and forth. "Shut up!" he screamed in his head and pushed himself up from the chair. He paced the room. "Semper idem—always the same." The voices were stronger now. He gathered the cloth strips piled at the foot of the chair and headed for the hidden hatch in the kitchen floor.

She heard the click above her head, and her heart-beat faster, knocking against her ribs trying to break through. Light beat down on her, blinding her so all she saw was a blaze before her. Suddenly, her hands were wrenched behind her and bound tightly, then her ankles, in the same manner. As her vision came back, it suddenly went dark again as she felt a soft material sliding across her eyes. Her captor held something against her mouth. It had a strong ammonia smell. She struggled slightly then passed out, the last thing she heard was a whisper saying, "Sorry."

He gathered her up in his arms and walked towards a large metal door. He threw the hatch and kicked open the door then, he entered a room furnished with a large metal sink on one side and a large metal cabinet on the other. In the middle of the room stood a large metal table with a sink on the end. He strode over to it and set Joyce down gently on top. Gathering a black satchel from the cabinet, he spread it open on a small side table set up beside her. Scalpels of various sizes lay

47

*side by side, glinting from the over-head light. A thin ice pick was cradled in a pad-
ded stand on the table. Beside it stood a burner, which he lit. Then gently, as if it
was a small child, he picked up the ice pick and set the tip in the flame, letting it
heat up to a glowing white. She lay silently in a deep sleep on top of the table. Her
breathing was deep and even, telling him he had time enough. Before he began,
he played Chopin lightly from the stereo. Slowly, with feather-light touches, he
cut her clothes off and tossed them into a bin against the wall behind him. He
rans his hands down her body and stroked her curves like a lover. Suddenly, a
voice screamed in his head and he stumbled back, gripping his head and moan-
ing. He crumpled on the floor into a fetal position, and the voices subsided to a
low thud. He breathed deeply to steady his heart, then slowly stretched out and
stood. He picked up his gloves and the ice pick and moved up to Joyce's head. With
the cloth still covering her eyes, he slowly lowered the tip and burned away the
cloth covering her left eye and quickly punctured it. The pick melted the eye into a
gooey mess, and she instantly woke up and started convulsing. Her body went into
spasms while he mirrored his actions to the right eye, and a scream escaped her. He
placed the pick on the table, then picked up a long, thin scalpel and ran his hand
between her breasts picking his spot. She felt nothing but the searing pain radiating through her head. Somewhere, in the background, she heard Chopin playing.
She didn't feel the cool metal pressed against her chest plate or the heat of his first
cut. The scalpel glided in smoothly as he worked it with a surgeon's fluidity. He
folded the skin back and picked up his bone saw. One by one, he cut her ribs and
set them aside exposing the lungs with the heart beating in its rhythmic motion
in between. Her breathing began to go shallow. There was a light gurgling sound.
He set the bone saw aside and picked up a small C-shaped clamp and secured it
over her left arm. He next connected a thin wire to the clamp and ran it into a
small portable computer. It detected the beating of her pulse and sent small shocks
into her system, which reduced the body's spasms. He picked up another scalpel,
a smaller one with a very thin blade, and began his cuts to the main arteries. The
heart completely slowed down to an irregular beat and stopped suddenly. Joyce's
life was no more. He disconnected the wire and clamp. After placing her heart in a
small cedar box, he cleaned up his scalpels and mopped up the blood that dripped.
He watched as the blood ran river-like down the table and into the drain on the
end. The voices had ceased in his head for the moment, but he knew that too soon,
they'd start up again stronger and louder than before.*

*   *   *   *

Bobby strolled into the precinct house at half past seven on one of the dark-
est and dreariest days he could remember in a long time. Leaning on the front

counter, he flashed Doris, the night dispatcher, his most winning smile. "How goes the night there, Doris my love?" Doris, a short, thin woman of fifty-four smiled back. "Not much. Domestic disputes, some young punks vandalizing a parked car, and a few B and E's." He patted her hand while kissing her cheek and continued on up to the homicide floor. After grabbing a coffee from the coffee machine, he headed to the thinking table. The bulletin board was covered with pictures and notes. He pulled down a picture of the first victim and sat at the table staring at it. That was how Gabe found him an hour later. "What's up, Bobby?" Startled, he jerked and glanced over his shoulder. "Christ, Gabe! Make some fuckin' noise next time."

"Sorry. Normally, you don't startle so easy." Bobby stretched and took a sip of his coffee, which he'd forgotten about. Grimacing, he set it back down and strode over to the window and stared out. Gabe knew him well enough to just wait him out. Whatever was on his mind, he'd eventually spit it out, so he settled back in a chair and watched Bobby stare out the window. "I'm unsettled, Nexs. This killer has me worried. We have two deaths of young, healthy women, and even as we speak, he's probably already killing again!" He turned and slammed his fist into his palm. Gabe relaxed in his chair, sighed and passed his coffee to Bobby. "I know what you mean, but what, my friend, are we going to do about it?" He grinned at him and a mischievous twinkle set in his eyes.

*   *   *   *

Groaning, she rolled out of bed, straight into her sometimes morning push-ups. Quickly, she did two sets of ten, then she jumped in the shower while waiting for her coffee to brew. Downstairs, she gathered up her ID and gun out of her safe and strolled out to her car. She had a few things she wanted to check out, and then she was going to go talk to Bobby and Gabe about a theory that had popped into her head late last night. She glided out of her driveway and headed downtown. She had a pretty good idea where Scrum would be right now, and if her luck held out, he would hopefully have some info for her.

She pulled into a parking lot outside a small, dumpy restaurant, cut her engine, and sat in her car, scoping out the people hanging around outside the doors. Spotting a short redhead in a tight checkered skirt and a very small tank top, she exited her car and leaned against it, waiting. She watched as the girl started towards her. "Ms. Velck, whaddaya want?" Hailey just smiled and motioned for her to follow. Once they were along the side of the building, she handed the girl a pack of smokes. "Seen Scrum today?"

"No." She pulled out a smoke and lit it, blowing the smoke in Hailey's face. "I need to ask you something, Trish, and I need the truth." The girl looked at her and kept on smoking. "The truth is just a bunch of bullshit anyway. Whaddaya want to know, Ms. Velck?"

"Have any of your customers requested any strange tricks lately?" Hailey didn't know Trish very well but what she did know was that this little girl had a very sharp mind; she also had extreme psychological problems. "That depends on the customer and on your definition of strange."

"Like new tools. Something with electric shocks and restraints." She saw a faint flicker in her eyes. Something about the question had sparked something in her. Trish started to get nervous "And what if they had?" she whispered, suddenly quite uncomfortable. Hailey looked at the girl worriedly "Has someone, Trish? Please, hon, I need to know if anyone has." She watched as the girl wrestled with her thoughts. "I wanna go somewhere. Take me there." She went around to the passenger side and settled herself.

*   *   *   *

He wrapped the body of the once lovely Joyce in a satin-lined wrap sheet, taking great care not to bruise her anywhere else on the body because he knew that some would show up on the body before long from the "controller," as he called it. The voices had begun a low drumming just behind his eyes. His sight wasn't very good, which he was grateful for, but his mind was clear. He cried silently. He felt like his heart was being crushed and his mind was soon to explode. Gathering her in his arms, he climbed the stairs and sat her at the table, closing the hatch. He walked to the sink and started to scrub his hands vigorously. There were no more tears, only coldness. Twisting the taps off, he turned and gathered Joyce back up in his arms and headed for the garage.

*   *   *   *

As they were pulling up to a breadbox-style house, Trish slinked out of the car before Hailey had even stopped. She watched as Trish walked up to the door and stood there for a minute staring. She opened the door and stepped inside. Hailey walked up behind her and went in, scanning the house while keeping a close eye on Trish. She led Hailey to the kitchen table and motioned for her to sit then left the room. Trish reemerged into the kitchen in a completely different outfit, which drastically changed her appearance. "Shocked, Ms. Velck?" Hailey shook her head. "Not really. I knew you played your game that way. Does it help, Trish? Changing your personality with each customer?" She smiled. "Let's get down to business. You wanted to know if any of my clients have gone freaky, on me right?" Hailey nodded. All right, then. Normally, I don't do the extreme, but a few of the other girls do. One of the girls, we'll call her Sue, had a client who strangled her while she was riding him. Another girl, we'll call her Beth, had a client who shocked her with some little computer contraption and pretended he was an alien. That's about as far as the freakiness has gotten."

"The client who used the computer contraption, is he a regular?" Trish shook her head. "No, he said that it would be his first time with a 'woman of this stature.' Those were his exact words."

"Do you know how he hooked it up to her?" Trish thought about it but shook her head. "I don't know. I never thought to ask her. What does this have to do with anyway?" Hailey ignored that question and asked her, "Have you spoken to Beth since?"

"The last time I talked to her was the day after. She has another job."

"Where else does she work?"

"Some little pub. I think it's called Trev's Place."

"Would you be able to describe the client's voice to me?"

"Sure. He was really quiet. His voice was almost whisper-like, with a thin accent. He sounded educated and rich. I could hear sadness in his voice, though. He creeped me out." Hailey filed the information away in her brain she'd write it down once she left. She wondered what Trish meant when she said he sounded rich. "Thanks. If you hear from Beth, would you please contact me? I don't suppose you'd tell me her real name?" Trish just smiled and walked with Hailey to the door. "If I don't hear from her tonight, I'll be in touch. Have a good day, Ms. Velck." She waved and got into her car. After pulling out her note-pad, she began jotting everything down that Trish had told her. She wasn't sure if this trail would lead her anywhere, but it was worth the travel.

*   *   *   *

Bobby and Gabe were heading down to the coroner's office at the exact moment Hailey left Trish's. Rye had phoned to tell them he had the results back from the lab. Bobby still had that twinkle in his eye, and Gabe was still wondering what was up his sleeve. "What's cooking in that head of yours, Stein?" Bobby grinned and pulled into the parking lot. "Let's go see what the doc has, shall we?" They walked down the hall and into Rye's office. Each simultaneously pulled out a chair and sat down.

"What's up, Doc?" Gabe grinned. Looking up from the file he was working on, Rye grinned back and handed him the file. "This is. The lab found nothing on the powder, but the bruising was caused by an electric shock shortly before death, not a major shock, just something to stabilize the body for a short time."

"The powder wasn't at all vital?" Bobby asked. Rye shook his head. "According to the lab, it was just a household powder ... you know, like baby powder or something." Gabe handed the file to Bobby "The bruising is interesting. Why would the killer want to shock his victims?"

"The victims were still alive when he started on their chest cavity. He probably used it to calm their bodies to keep them from convulsing." He swiveled around and grabbed a file. "The notes he left behind were written on plain, lined paper with a fine-tipped pen, black ink." He passed the file to Bobby. "I can have this copy?" Rye nodded. Gabe stood up, and Bobby followed suit. "Thanks, Doc. We'll talk to you later." Just as they were heading out the door, their beepers went off.

CHAPTER 11

Bobby sighed and turned around. "Can I use your phone, Doc?" He picked up the receiver and dialed in. "Stein here." The voice on the other end informed him he was needed at another scene. He gathered the necessary information and hung up. "Let's go, Nexs. There's been another one. Might as well come along, Doc. We'll just end up calling." Rye nodded and grabbed his coat. He pulled out his cell phone and called his team as they headed out the doors to the detectives' car. Bobby pulled his cell from the glove box and called Hailey. She picked up after the second ring. "Velck Investigations."

"It's Bobby. Heading out to another one. Meet us there?" He waited for her response. "Sure. Where am I going?" He relayed the directions to her and hung up. *Another one. That makes three.* Bobby slammed the steering wheel with the butt of his hand, causing Gabe to glance over at him. "You okay?" He nodded as he wove in between the traffic on the freeway.

*   *   *   *

"She's fresh, Detective. Only been exposed probably 'bout three hours ... four at max," the young cop relayed. Bobby nodded and kept walking. She was sprawled out on a small brown patch of grass surrounded by thin shrubs. The body was just being covered when Gabe and Bobby walked up with Hailey on their heels. "Wait a second, guys." Hailey shoved through the two of them and bent to look over the body while they talked with the uniforms. "Any ID found?" Bobby asked.

"No, sir. None on or around the body."

"Figured as much. Who found her?"

"A young guy. He was Roller-blading past with his dog when the dog went crazy and pulled him through the shrubs. Nobody else was around." Bobby jotted down the name and address and he and Gabe went to talk to Hailey. "Find anything new?" Hailey sat back on her heels, brushed off her hands, and stood. Just then, Rye strolled up. "Just in time, Doc." Gabe grinned and slapped him on the back. "Nothing new except that she's fresher than the last two, which could mean he's weakening. Same wounds as the other two, but I can't tell if there's a note this time." Bobby signaled to the forensic boys to get started. "We'll let them do their thing, and then we'll meet you in an hour or so at your office, Doc." Rye left to talk to the forensic team and Hailey, Gabe, and Bobby headed towards their cars. "Hailey, Gabe and I are going to go talk to the witness. Meet us at the morgue in an hour." They drove off in a cloud of dust. She went back to the scene. She stood watching the forensic people work. *What are you thinking? Where are you?* The questions flying around in her head were making her dizzy. Rye stood to the side watching her. He thought she looked cute standing there with her arms crossed and her one eyebrow cocked up. Walking over to her, he laid a hand on her shoulder, bringing her out of her trance. She glanced over at him and smiled. "You looked deep in thought there. Figure anything out?" They watched the team pack up the body and headed for their cars. "I'm getting there, I think. Headed to your office now?" He nodded, so she said she'd meet him there with a couple of sandwiches. She sat in her car for a few minutes. Scanning her notepad, she reviewed the last two murders and her conversation with the call girl. "Trev's Place" jumped out of the page at her, and she decided she'd stop by after the autopsy.

They were lounging in Rye's office, eating the sandwiches she had bought, when Bobby and Gabe walked in. "Have you two looked her over yet?" Bobby asked as he leaned against the door jamb. "Just about to get to her. We were waiting for the two of you." Hailey stood up and followed Rye out and down to the morgue suite. Rye and Hailey donned scrubs. Rye handed the detectives gloves and face masks. The morgue attendant wheeled the body out. With Hailey's help, Rye placed her on the autopsy table while the attendant set up the recording device and the doctor's tools, whispered something to Rye, and vacated to a small room off the suite.

"Shall we get started? Hailey, will you please take notes?" He asked handing her the clipboard, and started the visual exam. "Date is June 18 of the year 2002. Time is 5:45 pm. Case file 4679. Victim visual exam." Bobby and Gabe stood off to the side while he dictated to Hailey the state in which the body appeared. The head itself was not damaged, but where the eyes should have been, there was nothing but a pair of charred holes. The other two victims' eyes had also burnt out too, but there was also major head trauma. The neck was bruised, most likely from a restraint. It was the same with her wrists and ankles. There was also a small bruise on her upper arm about the same size as a quarter. The chest area disturbed Bobby a great deal. Her ribs were ripped apart in the same fashion as the other two, and the heart had been removed with smooth, even slice marks across the main arteries. Rye could not find a jagged edge on either ventricles.

Hailey took close-up pictures of the chest cavity; the eyes; the bruising at the neck, wrist, and ankles; and the small bruise on her upper arm. They then began their internal exam with Bobby and Gabe looking on. Suddenly, a cell phone rang, breaking Rye's concentration. All three of them reached for their jacket pockets, Hailey flipped hers open and talked quickly into it, then hung up just as quickly. "Sorry." She sent Rye an apologetic smile and started writing again. "Anything we need to know Hailey?" Gabe asked. She kept her back turned while she thought about telling them what she was up to but decided against it. "Don't worry about it, Gabe." He furrowed his brow at her back. He didn't believe her but decided it wouldn't help to bug her about it. He glanced at Bobby but couldn't read his expression. He was staring at the body, almost like he was in a trance. So Gabe snapped his fingers in front of his face. Bobby kind of shook his head and looked at Gabe. "What?"

"Are you okay? Maybe we should go get something to eat and some coffee." He nodded. "Good idea. Doc, we're going to go eat. Call us when you're done. Meet us at the precinct, Hailey, in about two hours." They threw away their gloves and masks and headed upstairs. "Why do morgues always have to be in a basement?" Gabe grumbled as they ascended the stairs. "A big guy like you scared of a little basement?" Bobby teased as they walked to the car. "Where do you wanna chow, Nexs?" Gabe suggested the deli off Mercer Way.

*　*　*　*

Hailey left Rye's office about twenty-five minutes later and headed out to the pub Trish had told her about. She arrived about twenty minutes later and entered through a wooden door carved with an entr'acte design. She stood just to the side of the door while she gave the place a quick scan. There was an old man sitting at the far end chatting with the bartender, while over to her right, in the far corner, there was a group of young guys conversing over a couple of jugs of beer. Every now and then, they would let out a hoot of victory over the basketball game being shown on the TV. Hailey decided to grab a stool at the bar but first went to the washroom. When she came out, the place was busier than before with more people flowing in.

"Welcome. Don't think I've ever seen you in here before. New to town?" Trevor asked the woman who had just plopped onto a stool. He gave her a quick study while waiting for her reply. "No, I've lived here a few years now, but I've never been in here before. It's very … quaint with a modern style to it." Trevor smiled. "Thank you. I was going for an old comfy look with a bit of modernism. So, what's your poison?" Hailey smiled at him. She liked this man who smiled so easily that it made her want to smile more often. "I'll have a pint of Keith's please." He nodded and started to pour. Hailey studied the people filling the place through the glass behind the bar. There was a wide assortment, and quite obviously most of them knew the waitress, because she was getting mauled left, right, and center but seemed to be enjoying it by the smile plastered on her face when she came up to the bar. "Trev, hon, can I get three Rickard's, six shots of rye, and one double white rum and Coke." He nodded, dropped off Hailey's beer, and began pouring drinks. She watched him pour. He brought the drinks to the waitress and loaded up her tray. Hailey caught his attention, and he slid over to her. "Another one then?" he asked. She shook her head, "I'd like to talk to you about one of your employees." She showed him her ID and her PI license. He looked at her strangely for a moment then signaled to Courtney. "I'll be in the back. Can you handle the taps and floor for a few minutes?" She nodded, and he motioned for Hailey to follow him. He led her to a small office in the back of the pub through the kitchen where a skinny cook was dancing around to Travis Tritt. Trevor laughed at him and shut the office door. He pulled out a chair for Hailey then leaned against the desk instead of sitting behind it. "How can I help you … Ms. Velck, wasn't it?"

"Hailey, please. I have a few questions for you about a possible employee. The only problem is I don't know her real name. I only know her as Beth." Hailey described the victim's hair color, height, and approximate age to the bartender and studied his face while waiting for his answer. "Sounds like Joyce. Is she in trouble?"

"When was the last time you saw her?"

"Yesterday. She closed the pub with me. She was here till a little after one in the morning." Hailey wrote everything down. "Did she walk home?" He nodded. "Where does she live?"

"She lives down the street from here. Head a block and a half to the left, and look for an apartment complex called …" He snapped his fingers. "Kork or something. You can't miss it because it has a very large spruce bush smack dab in the middle of the yard." Trevor watched her scribble. "Look, is Joyce in trouble or what? I care about her, and if she needs help, well …" Hailey looked at this man sitting in front of her. She noticed the crease of worry over his brow and the light sheen of sweat that panic sometimes caused, covering his face. His eyes were dark, and he looked at her expectantly, waiting. "Can you take a ride with me? Anyone who can cover for about an hour?" He nodded and dialed a number on the phone beside him. A fewseconds later, he quickly chatted with someone named Harry and asked him to cover for him at the pub, then he hung up. About twenty minutes later, she was ushering him into Rye's office and into a chair. He looked at her dumbstruck. "Why are we here?"

"The doctor will tell you when he gets here." She turned and faced the corner and made a call on her cell phone. He heard her mumble something into the phone and hang it up. Then she walked over to the window behind the desk and stood with her back to him just starring out the window. He was getting really pissed off and scared as well. Why wouldn't she tell him anything? Was Joyce dead? God, he hoped not. Just then, the door opened and a doctor glided in. "What the hell is going on?" Trevor asked the six-foot-four-inch man in the white coat. Rye held out his hand and introduced himself. "I'm Dr. Jackson. You must be Trevor Amore. I know you must be frustrated right now, what with being dragged down here in the middle of your day. We'd like you to view a body and tell us if it is in fact your employee." Trevor collapsed into a chair. View a body? This must be some elaborate joke. No, nobody he knew would be this cruel. He stood up and solemnly followed the doctor. They stopped beside a large window with the blinds closed. Hailey placed a hand on his shoulder while Rye disappeared behind the door beside the window. Trevor was in shock. Would it be Joyce behind the blinds? If it was, then what? If it wasn't, then what? The blinds started to open slowly. He felt the PI's hand drop just as the blinds were fully opened, and he was staring down the length of a white sheet draped over a body. The doctor motioned to his assistant, and the little man folded back the top of the sheet revealing the face of Joyce Yuckermin. Trevor's legs went weak, and he slumped against the window. He felt sick. The assistant covered her back up and wheeled her out a set of swinging doors on the other side of the little room. Rye came out and helped Trevor into a chair. "Joyce. That's Joyce," he whispered in a rasp. Hailey called Bobby and told him the victim had been identified. He told her they'd meet them in Rye's office. "I'm sorry, Mr. Amore, but we need to talk some more. There are a couple of detective's on their way that need to speak with you." She signaled to Rye to head up to his office. Together, they helped him to his feet and back to the office where he just slouched in a chair. Rye's assistant brought Trevor some tea and dropped off some papers. Hailey stood by the window, while Rye got a few vitals from Trevor. Outside, Bobby and Gabe pulled up and almost ran to the building. Two minutes later, they barged into the office. Introductions were made and, questions immediately asked. In short order, Bobby had the victim's home address and next of kin. He thanked him then motioned Hailey out into the hall. Once the door was shut, he asked her what was up. "Where'd you find him?" She counted to ten. "I found him in a pub called Trev's Place.

Ever been there?" He shook his head no. "How did you find the pub?" He knew she wouldn't tell him but asked anyway. She studied him. "Let's just say a little birdie led me in the right direction."

CHAPTER 12

"A little birdie huh? Figured as much. Well, at least we're one step closer now. We have a name and an address, so let's get rolling." Hailey took Trevor back to his pub and met up with the detectives at the victim's address. When she got up to the apartment, there were uniforms everywhere. She found Bobby in the middle of the tiny living room, talking to the landlord who was staring everywhere in utter amazement. "When was the last time you saw the tenant?" The landlord was a tiny man, in his early sixties, Hailey guessed. He was wearing big bottle-cap glasses that enlarged his eyes to about ten times the normal size. He looked at Bobby, who towered over him by four feet. He blinked, making him look almost cartoonish. "I'm not sure. Maybe yesterday? What day is it?" Bobby looked at him in exasperation, "It's Tuesday." The old man nodded. "Yup, I saw her yesterday then. In the morning, she likes to jog in the park behind the building. Nice girl, she is. She's not in trouble? She didn't seem like a trouble-maker, and I can spot them anywhere." Bobby thanked him and led him to the door. "She didn't come home last night," the old man stated as he was leaving, Bobby stopped him. "What did you say?"

"I said she didn't come home last night. She always says good night when she comes in from work. I told you she was a nice girl." He turned and walked down the hall and disappeared into the elevator. Hailey stood beside Bobby watching him. "Hey." She snapped her fingers in front of his face. "You all right?" He walked back to the living room. "She was taken last night right after work. The killer must have been waiting for her. He had her picked before he took her." Hailey nodded. "Premeditation. Thought before the action. This one was cleaner than the last two. I have other info that might interest you. She lived a double life, Bobby. Maybe the other two did also." He stared at her. A double life? "Whaddaya mean?"

"She was a call girl. She worked for a company named 'Dream Fantasy.' I know the owner."

"You know the owner of an escort service? Pray tell?" Bobby asked her. "I met her last year. That's all I'll tell you."

"Wait a minute. How did you know to go to her?"

"She's one of my snitches, as you guys in blue call them. I'll introduce the two of you ... but just you." He nodded. "Okay ... when?" She watched the officers bag and tag around the apartment. "I'll let you know. She's a bit temperamental."

"Well, let's hurry on it, because I have a feeling we'll be seeing another victim sooner than the last one." Hailey nodded in agreement, and they went into the victim's bedroom where Gabe was going through every drawer of her dresser. "Find anything that might be useful, Nexs?" He pointed to the bed as he closed the last drawer. "Found her diary and an address book. Nothing else useful." Wearing gloves, Hailey picked up the address book and flipped through the pages. The pages were color coded and covered in neat, flowing writing. She only had a few friends with Seattle numbers. Flipping to the back pages, she found little notes jotted down: *Buy milk and bread. Call Mom tomorrow.*" Her work schedule for the pub was written down. She flipped a few more pages and came across what looked like jumbled-up words. She frowned at them. "*10-sun-mik, 5-fr-jef, 12-mo-jed.*" She pulled out her notepad and wrote them down. She showed Bobby. "Maybe her schedule for the escort service?" she said. Bobby shrugged. "Look into it, and I'll phone the numbers listed in her book." They left the apartment a few minutes later and went to the precinct.

Hailey went back to the little house to talk with Trish. She knocked on the door and heard some movement on the other side. The door opened a crack, and Hailey saw one blue eye look out. The next minute, she was standing in the little kitchen watching Trish putter around the stove. "Sorry to interrupt, but I was wondering if you'd answer a few more questions for me?" She gestured Hailey into a chair and placed a plate of eggs in front of her. "Questions again, Ms. Velck? How about some coffee?" She turned and pulled a mug down from a cupboard. "Cream and sugar?" Hailey nodded. "Both, please." She scooped up some eggs on her fork and took a bite. She almost sighed out loud; she had never tasted eggs this good before. "What's in these? They're excellent."

"A little of this, a little of that." She waved the question away. "Is that what you came here for?" Hailey smiled. "Not exactly. It's about Beth aka Joyce." Hailey watched for a reaction at the mention of the name. She noticed a slight recognition in her eyes. "I went to that pub you told me about. The police found a body last night. I brought Trevor in to identify it. He identified the body as Joyce Yuckermin, a waitress at the pub." Trish rose from the table and walked to the sink. She poured her coffee down the drain, then just stood there. "I should have told you her real name. I just didn't think anything could happen, you know." She turned and faced Hailey again. "What do you need to know?"

Hailey nodded and pulled out her note-pad. "I need you to tell me what this means." She pointed to the coded writing she had jotted down from Joyce's address book. Trish took the pad and studied the writing. She paced a bit and chewed on her lip, mumbling to herself. "Of course! These are her regulars. The clients that prefer her and the days she sees them. See here …" She pointed to the first one. "This means Mike at ten on Sunday, then Jeff at five on Friday, and Jed at twelve on Monday." She handed back the pad and sat down again. "I probably have their phone numbers and addresses. Actually not probably, I do have them." She got up again and disappeared down the hall only to return a few minutes later with a sheet of paper that she handed to Hailey, "These are the numbers and addresses. I can't guarantee that these are real, but it's what I have and all I can do to help." Hailey nodded and stood. "I'm sure it'll help. Thanks." She left.

CHAPTER 13

He wandered around in a daze on the tenth floor of the top law firm in Seattle. His coworkers greeted him as he passed but he hardly noticed. A short blond woman called out to him, but he kept walking. She started to chase him down the hall and stopped him just before he could close his office door. "Sir, there's a board meeting in ten minutes, and these are all your messages." He took the little pink pieces of paper and shut the door in her face. He headed straight for the mini-bar, pouring himself a Scotch and water, then moving to the large Edwardian-style desk in front of a wall of windows and sitting down in a deep red swivel chair. He tossed the messages onto his desk, watching them flutter down and scatter. Spinning his chair around, he threw back the last of his Scotch and the images of the women flooded back into his head. He dropped the glass and fumbled with his desk drawer, pulling it open and grabbing some of his pills, trifluoperazine. He threw four down his throat dry and gripped his head till they started to work. Naked flesh and blood ran through his mind until, five minutes later, the images started to fade, and then they were gone. He slowly raised his head and gazed out the window; everything was a haze again.

There was a light tapping on his door, and then it opened with a little swish. The short blond stuck her head in and reminded him that he was supposed to be at the board meeting. He stood up and nodded, and she left the room. He splashed cold water on his face and straightened his tie. He grabbed his note-pad and headed to the boardroom.

He walked through a set of oak doors and into a room of glass. The pills he had taken brought his mind to a light, hazy state, and his movements were slow. His eyes had a dim, glassy look to them, and a slight smile flirted with his mouth. He slid slowly into a high-back chair amongst twelve others that surrounded a large dark table. Once seated, he scanned the faces around him. All were older men with varying degrees of graying hair. Names floated through his mind as each face settled. The man at the head of the table started to talk to him. "Glad you could join us. We haven't seen much of you lately. Problems?" He shook his head no. "No problems, Mr. Squire, just some intense clients." He stood up and went to a glass

62

bar set up at the end of the room, poured himself some water, then just stood there drinking it while the rest of the table discussed cases and such. His eyes wandered the room. He had always liked this room with its walls of glass. It reminded him that he was free again.

*   *   *   *

Hailey and Bobby were seated at the thinking table going over all three victim's files while Gabe was placing pins on a map where each body was found. "What do we know so far? The first was a part-time hooker and waitress. Fair hair and skin, medium height. The second was a full-time waitress with fair hair and skin and the third was a part-time call girl and a part time waitress with fair hair and skin also. Obviously, he has a preference. We can assume the fourth, if there is a fourth, will fall into the same category." Hailey nodded. "The perp is very careful with the bodies, leaving no evidence at the scene or on the bodies, but he deposits them where they're sure to be found. That action shows guilt so perhaps he's a little off his rocker. We should check out mental hospitals. See if there have been any releases in the last five years. Look for past criminal offences such as anything dealing with sexual abuse to women or beatings." Gabe nodded. "I'll start on it. You guys hungry?"

"Grab me a sandwich and a V8," Bobby asked. Hailey shook her head. "Nothing for me, thanks." He left the room. "What makes you think the killer is a psycho?" Hailey stood up and stretched. They'd been sitting at that table for nearly three hours now, and it felt more like ten, but they weren't any further than they were when they entered the room. "I don't think the killer is psycho, Stein, but I do feel that he probably has, at some point, spent some time either in a mental facility or at least has seen a psychiatrist. I'll look into the shrink part of my theory, and you two can look into the hospital records. We'll talk tomorrow." She grabbed her jacket off the back of her chair then left with a sudden rush that left Bobby staring after her. Two minutes later, while he was still trying to figure out what had gotten into her, Gabe came back with the sandwiches and phone numbers for mental hospitals. "This all you could find?" Gabe rolled his eyes. "You'll have to settle for tuna and orange juice today, partner." Bobby grumbled something about the vending machine but ate it anyway. "Where did Hailey go?"

"She left. She's gone to look into shrinks. Says she'll talk to us tomorrow," Bobby mumbled around the food in his mouth. "These numbers are only for the south and east sides. You take south, and I'll take east." They both picked up their phones and started dialing.

*   *   *   *

The meeting had ended, and he was back in his office. His secretary informed him that he had a one o'clock appointment and asked if he was okay because he looked a little pale. What she failed to mention was that besides looking pale, he also had a distant stare in his eyes and a gleam that disturbed her even though she couldn't say why. He heard someone call his name. It was distant. It sounded painful, like it was suffering and it made him stand up abruptly, knocking over his chair. He stood very still, listening intently. There it was again, a faint crying of his name coming from somewhere in his office. He followed the sound and ended up staring at himself in the mirror only it wasn't just himself he saw. The face looking back at him was pale and sunken with glazed eyes and a strange-looking grin. He touched his face and felt himself touching it, but he couldn't change the expression. Suddenly, the voice screamed in his head causing him to groan and sink to the floor. He curled up, clutching his head while the voice battered at him.

"Kill the little blonde because she knows," it kept repeating. "She knows! She knows! Kill her! Kill her!"

He sobbed so quietly he wasn't sure if it was actually him. The voice roared and made him whimper in pain. He pulled himself over to his desk, grasping for his pills. "Kill her!" Then blackness enveloped him, and the voice grew quiet.

He awoke a few minutes later sprawled on the floor. Slowly, he pulled himself into his chair. What had happened? Suddenly, it came flashing back so rapidly that he had to make a quick dash for the bathroom before his lunch came up on his desk. He staggered out of the bathroom. Swallowing three of his pills, he told his secretary to cancel all of his appointments for the rest of the day. "Sir, your one o'clock is already here." He told her to send them away and reschedule. He gave himself a few minutes, then he grabbed his coat and his briefcase and left his office. His secretary told him that Mr. Squire would like to see him. He headed for the associate's office, pausing outside the door. He knocked and then walked in. Mr. Squire sat behind a huge mahogany desk in front of a beautiful view of Lake Washington. The older man motioned for him to sit. "Are you done for the day?" He nodded yes and said he wasn't feeling well after all. "You do look pale, pale and tired. Maybe you should take a few days off, humm? Would that help? I feel that you're having some problems. Am I correct in thinking that?" He started to sweat a little. "I'm just not feeling well, really. There's no need to concern yourself, sir." The older man studied him for a few minutes. He noticed the black circles around his eyes, the paleness, the glazed eyes, and a strange glint as well. He knew very little about his childhood but knew that he had gone through hell to get where he was now. It would be a shame if it all came crashing down on him. "All right then, but if you need to talk, you know where you can find me." He nodded and assured him he'd be fine. Once outside, he breathed deeply like he had been short of air. The pills were kicking in, and by the time he made it to his house, he could hardly function. He crawled into bed and instantly fell asleep.

*   *   *   *

When Hailey left the guys, she went back to her office and booted up her computer. She had decided it would be easier if she just hacked into the files she needed to look at and if her attempts failed, then she would contact Ramsey and beg him, if necessary, to help her around all the red tape protecting medical files. She sent her fingers flying over the keyboard, setting up her blocks in case she was detected snooping around. Crashing through some very tight security walls, Hailey quickly found the files and downloaded them into a special folder. In a matter of ten minutes, she had copied every file pertaining to the area of severe mental and emotional problems. She snuck out of the system the same way she got in, covering any trail she might have left and returned to her main screen. She stood up and poured some tea then paced the room a bit. Once she had organized her thoughts, she opened up the downloaded file and began to skim it, looking for psychotic disorders that dealt mainly with delusions, thought disturbances, and poverty of thought perhaps some emotional outbursts as well. She quickly narrowed her search down to about fifty files and deleted the rest, making sure to erase them completely from the hard drive. She then printed out all fifty of the remaining files and erased the downloaded file. She shut down her computer, closed up her office, and went upstairs with tea in one hand and the printed files in the other. Stepping into the kitchen, she tossed the files on to the table then went to her stereo and pushed play. Paula Cole flowed out of the speakers engulfing her with smooth sounds. She let herself be lulled for a few minutes then brought herself back and went into the kitchen to make herself some dinner and go through the files. She knew she had a full night ahead of her, so she threw on some coffee too.

*   *   *   *

Back at the precinct, Bobby and Gabe were still working the phone lines with the search of the hospital records. "Damn it!" Gabe slammed the receiver down. "Every person says the same thing, 'Patient files are confidential, sir,' then hangs-up on you." He stretched then glanced at his watch. "Shit, it's midnight already. I'm going home. Talk to you in the morning, Bobby." He stood, threw on his jacket, and stalked out of the squad room. Bobby sent him a wave then finished his phone call. He had had about as much luck as Gabe and decided it was a dead end. He stretched and went over to the coffee machine. He was staring out the window when the dispatcher buzzed him. "Detective, I just got a 911 call about a body in the Newport Hills Park. Caller was a young male with a female. I told them to stay put and sent out two cars." He grabbed his jacket and headed for the car. In four minutes, he was at Gabe's front door. Ten minutes after that they were headed towards the body.

CHAPTER 14

The body was found under an oak tree about three feet from the path. The victim was lying twisted with her upper half face down and her lower half toes up. When Bobby and Gabe arrived on the scene, two patrolmen had sealed off the surrounding area where a small and curious crowd had started to form. He always thought it odd how, regardless of the hour, murder scenes always drew a crowd. Gabe went to talk to the cops while he headed for the victim. Tommy and his team were already there, so he went to get his take on it. "Tommy, what do you see?" Tommy shook Bobby's hand. "Early thirties, blond, about five-eight with a small tattoo on her left ankle. She's partially clothed in a dark skirt and one shoe. An Italian pump, very pricey, I might add. Hasn't been here longer than a few hours. We haven't moved her yet, so I don't know how she died. Thought you'd probably want to have a look before we rolled her." Bobby was squatted next to her left ankle, examining what looked like a butterfly. He pulled out his penlight and looked closer. It was a small butterfly settled on a colorful flower. He stood up and motioned for them to roll her over. The victim had been brutalized. Her face was covered in blood and dirt, and her chest was spread wide open with muscle and tissue hanging and the lungs visible. "The heart's missing. Pass me a pair of gloves, would you?" Tommy handed him some. He brought out his penlight again. The aorta was smooth where it had been cut as were the vena cava and the pulmonary vein. He moved his light up to her face, where it made the blood glint at him. The eyes were burnt, and melted flesh mixed with the jelly substance seeping out of the socket on a trail of blood. Standing up, he put his penlight away and tossed the gloves. Gabe walked over to him and repeated what the cop had told him. "It's our guy. He's getting sloppy, though. She's still got her skirt on, and she's fresh. I think he might have killed her outside because her right foot is scuffed with dirt, but not the same dirt she's lying in. It's lighter." They watched Tommy and his team, bag and snap pictures. "Are you calling Hailey tonight?"

"No, I'll call her in a few hours after the doc has a look." He glanced to his right and watched as the medical examiner's van pulled up. Gabe stood scanning the crowd that had gained in excess since their arrival. He noted two-teen age males dressed in baggy jeans and hooded sweatshirts, a young Mexican couple, a group of drunk, middle-aged men, and an old homeless man. He felt as if someone was watching him, but he couldn't find the source. A chill ran up his spine, and his hand snaked to his gun. "Gabe, let's go." Bobby tapped him on the shoulder.

They arrived at the morgue before the body, so they went to Rye's office to find him. "Doc, did you get the call?" He nodded. "I was just about to go down to the exam room. Is she here yet?" Bobby shook his head. "No, we beat them here, but they shouldn't be long." They followed Rye out and down to the delivery room where the medical techs were just unloading the body on to a stretcher. Rye signed their clipboard and talked to his assistant who started to wheel the body into exam room three. He then motioned Bobby and Gabe to follow him and went in after the body. "Are we waiting for Hailey?" Rye asked as he pulled on gloves. "No. Just start, and I'll call her." Fifteen minutes later, she walked into the exam room just as Rye was logging the stomach contents. She walked over to Bobby and Gabe, and they filled her in on what they knew. "He's breaking down. We found her partially clothed and her feet were dirty. There was no note either." She nodded and walked over to Rye. "Mind if I take a look?" He looked up. "Not at all. Perhaps you'll find something I missed."

"I doubt that." She pulled on some gloves and started to search with her hands and eyes. Rye stepped back and watched. He noticed how her eyes took on a sort of hazy sheen and her brow creased while her lips went slack. Then, just as suddenly, she was tossing the gloves away and walking over to the detectives. "He killed her first this time, before he burnt out her eyes. He's getting weaker. Do we have an ID yet?" They looked at Rye. "It should be back from the lab shortly along with her tox-screen. She had a very expensive meal about two hours before she was killed."

"Expensive? Like what, lamb chops or somethin'?" Gabe asked.

"It's too digested to tell for sure, but I did find remnants of caviar," he said as he walked to the sink. "Let's go to my office."

"Okay. What do we know? We know that victim four is, shall we say, of a higher class than the first three. So ..." Bobby paced back and forth, desk to door and back again, twisting a cigar between his fingers. "How do we know she's of a higher class?" Gabe asked. Hailey piped up. "Because of her shoe for one thing. Armani isn't cheap, and her body was smooth. Exceptionally so! Meaning that she pampered herself frequently, and spas are not cheap my friend, and lastly, her shredded skirt. Finely hand-sewn moth silk skirt. More than likely ordered from Europe." They all blinked at her. "Well, okay then," Gabe spat dumbfounded. Hailey just smiled at them.

"So now we need to find her name. Doc?" Rye picked up his phone and punched a number then spoke softly and hung up. Two minutes later, a short man in a lab coat walked in and handed him a folder and walked back out.

"Madelyn Groves. Age thirty-two. Resides in Georgetown on South Bennett Street. Not married and no children." He handed the file to Bobby. "I'll finish up with the body and get her cleaned up while you guys find the family." Rye stood up and left them sitting in his office. "Let's go back to my office." Hailey stood up and headed for the parking lot.

*   *   *   *

Why her? Why did it have to be her? It was sloppy. She kept one shoe and her skirt, so soft, wouldn't come off. Where did I kill her? He remembered dragging her soft, beautiful body through the dirt. "I scraped her heels, I know it!"

"You did good. You killed the lying bitch. She got what she deserved."

He grabbed his head and moaned. Each time the voices talked, his head pounded like there were hundreds of little men with hammers bashing the insides of his skull over and over again. He groped in the dark for his pills, knocking over his Scotch, he grasped the pill bottle, shook out three, and swallowed them dry. He lay back and closed his eyes. Bright red, violent flashes of the brutal slaying sprayed across his once-black vision. As the flashes danced in his eyes, he curled into a ball and cried silently into his pillow until, finally, he passed out.

*   *   *   *

"One of you needs to go notify next of kin." She looked from Bobby to Gabe. "I'll go. You guys dig some more into those psychiatric files." Gabe went out the deck door, leaving the two of them staring after him. "Odd that he would volunteer himself." Bobby shrugged his shoulders and began flipping through the files in front of him. Hailey turned to her computer and began a new search for psychotic behavior files. The pile Bobby was looking through was the ones she'd downloaded earlier but seeing the new victim's body had made her itchy. Two to four years back in the files wasn't going to get them anywhere. Bobby glanced over at her where she was hunched over her keyboard with her face mere inches in front of the screen scowling. He slid his chair beside her to see just what she was scowling at. What he saw was not what he expected. Her fingers were flying like lightning over the board while numbers and letters ran across the screen. It all looked like gibberish to Bobby, but he knew that whatever she was doing was illegal. Suddenly, there was a flash across the screen and then they were looking at confidential and sealed files of the FBI psychiatric department. "What the fuck, Hailey?" he whispered. She turned her head and looked him dead in the eyes. "You want to catch the bastard, don't you?" He nodded. "Then pretend you never witnessed that." She turned back to the screen and began printing files that dated back twenty to thirty years. Bobby started to group them in their respective piles, and Hailey got up to make some tea and coffee because it looked like they were going to be at it all night.

Four hours later, they were still pouring through files. Gabe had shown up around two hours earlier and picked up the pace easily. She was reading a file that dated back forty-three years ago.

The subject was a male ten-year-old who was institutionalized after he was found lying with his brutalized mother's body in his home. He was first left in the custody of his aunt who, only three months later, had him committed to a Catholic psychiatric hospital. She claimed that he had attacked her in her sleep with a pillow, but once she woke up and struggled, he dropped to the floor like a rag doll. Then of all things, she locked him in his room and called the Catholic priest at her church who hurried over to calm her and phone the authorities. The priest repeated what the aunt had told him to the police officer and then again to the doctor that came to examine the boy.

For the next three years, the boy was tested, poked, and prodded but stayed in a sort of comatose state. Then one morning, a nurse went into his room to find him sitting up in bed looking around the room. She told the doctors that he had spoken to her briefly but she was too stunned to remember what he had said. She did remember the look he had in his eyes. She told the doctors that it had given her the creeps and sent her running from the room. The doctor calmed the hysterical nurse and sent her home. He then entered the boy's room, at which time the child was standing facing the covered window. The doctor announced himself and waited for a reply, but instead of speaking, the boy turned to face him and raised his arm in what looked to be a forced movement. Hailey looked up from the file. The clock was telling her it was midnight, and by the deep rumble of Gabe's snoring, it sounded like he had been out for awhile. She was amazed that it hadn't interrupted her reading. She scanned the rest of the office but saw no Bobby, so she stood up and stretched her bones and headed for the kitchen. Halfway down the hallway, she stopped and breathed in deeply. What was that heavenly scent? Oh God, was she ever hungry! She slipped into the kitchen without a sound and snuck up behind him. "What's cookin'?"

"Give a guy a heart attack, why don't cha!" He gripped the counter heaving. Hailey held her gut, roaring with laughter. Bobby, finally getting his breathing under control, "It's my secret omelet, you sneaky little ..." She gave him a quick kick, to the knee dropping him. "No need for name-calling. Smells great!" She held her hand out. He looked up at her grinning face and pushed himself up. "I guess I'll share since this is your house." He slung his arm around her neck and led her to the table. "Did the giant bear wake up at all?" Hailey laughed and shook her head no. "We'll let him sleep but cook one up for him anyways. We'll stick it under his nose when we go back there." Bobby placed a plate in front of her that smelt of herbs, veggies, and cheese and made her mouth water instantly.

CHAPTER 15

Madelyn Groves had worked in one of the many top law firms in Seattle. Hailey found her desk on the tenth floor. She sat down in the chair and scanned the surroundings. There was constant activity on the floor with people rushing in and out of offices and constant chatter. Suits were everywhere she looked. She leaned back in the chair and looked through the office door just behind her. There was no one in it at the moment. She decided that if no one was in it when she was done here, then she was going to snoop around it. For what, she wasn't sure. She looked at her watch. Bobby and Gabe were planning to talk to people downstairs then, work their way up. She figured she had about half an hour till they showed up. She pulled open the bottom, right drawer and started looking through it. Why this woman? That question kept popping into her head. The first three victims were quiet, homely types, but this victim was an assistant in a law firm. Where was the connection? She stood up and glared down at the top of the desk. The drawers revealed nothing but law talks, pencils, and things necessary for a woman to get through her day. The top of the desk was very tidy with files piled on the edge and a picture of a woman and child at the edge of the desk. A computer and keyboard sat at the right, top corner but only held basic filing programs, no connection to the Internet or anything useful. Hailey entered the office and shut the door behind her. Leaning against it, she scanned the room. It was very spacious with a sitting area to the right and a small bathroom tucked into one corner. To her right was a high maple wood bar stocked with Scotch, vodka, and gin and crystal goblets instead of the usual glass. The wall behind the bar was mirror from floor to ceiling with track lighting glaring down on the top of the bar making the crystal dance. Directly in front of her was a desk. It was a deep red Edwardian Renaissance desk. She walked towards it, conscious of any movement or sound that wasn't her own. She went to the desk chair but stopped just short of it and stared out the high floor-to-ceiling windows. The view was amazing. She could see clearly over the rooftops of some of the buildings and the glint of the sun reflecting off the buildings taller than the one she was in. The sky was a smooth palette of blue with wisps of white scattered throughout. She dragged her eyes away and pulled out the deep red chair and settled herself. What was she looking for? Why did she enter this office? These questions danced through her mind while she scanned the top of the desk. It was very neat, almost as if it was never used. There was a pen holder on the edge beside an old picture of a family. A computer took up the left side of the desk, while on the right side were a phone and intercom and an area with a very thin pile of files on it. The desk was equipped with three drawers, one large one on either side and one thin drawer directly in front of Hailey's stomach. She faced the computer and booted it up. A password entry window jumped out at her. She randomly started to enter words, letters, and numbers to no avail. Frustrated, she started searching the thin drawer for a clue to the password or the password itself. Nothing jumped at her so she moved to the other two drawers and came up empty-handed again. She sighed and looked longingly at the screen. She shut the computer off and stood up pushing the chair in. If she only had more time. She left the office just in time to see Bobby and Gabe step off the elevator. She walked to meet them half-way, all the while aware of eyes from every cubicle trained on her and the two men. "Did you find anything in her desk?" Bobby asked once they met up with her. She shook her head. "Nothing that would help find who did this. What about you two, anybody have anything interesting to say?"

"Nothing concrete. Just the usual office gossip. She was sleeping with her boss and yadda yadda. Nobody told us anything pertaining to her murder."

"While I was searching her desk, I did print up her home address." She pulled a printout out of her pocket and handed it to Bobby. He scanned it, then stuffed it in his pocket. It was the same address that the doc had given him. "She lives in Georgetown, on South Bennett Street. Hailey and I'll go check out her place, Gabe, you stay and finish interviewing this floor then meet us back at the station house in about two hours." Hailey and Bobby went to the elevator, and Gabe headed in the opposite direction. Once in the car, Bobby turned the radio, on and Hailey ran through her mental evidence again. The first three victims were close in age, build, and life-style. The fourth victim was older and more refined, with a life style suitable to the higher class. The first three were found in public places with no clothing or clues. The fourth was left with one shoe and her skirt but also in a public place. The first three were planned, but the fourth gave the air of sloppiness. The killer was rushed. He's getting weak, she thought to herself. There'll be at least one more death. She was sure of it. Bobby pulled into the drive of a brilliant old red-brick house. The drive was littered with flowers of every shape, size, and dizzying color. The yard looked as if it ran on for miles behind and to the sides. There were tall elms to the far left and short fat shrubs to the right. They pulled up to the house. Hailey slid out of the car. They walked up to the door, and Bobby pushed the bell. About three minutes later, the door opened to a stately old woman with hair as white as snow twisted up into a tight bun. She wore a light dusting of makeup and an expensive cream-colored suit. Hailey gave her a smile, and to her surprise, the woman, returned it. Bobby introduced himself and Hailey and the woman invited them in. Hailey took in everything at once. The entry-way was the size of two regular-size living rooms and had wood flooring. There was a wall-size mirror to their right, and straight ahead of them was a twisting staircase. The woman led them into what Hailey could only call a parlor. They seated themselves with the woman in a high-back chair and Hailey and Bobby across from her on a surprisingly comfortable Victorian couch. "Madam," Bobby started. "We're sorry to have to meet you this way." The woman nodded, and a young man entered the room with a tray of tea and coffee and quietly set it down on the small table between them. Hailey offered to pour, and the woman thanked her. She poured tea for the two of them and coffee, black, for Bobby. "We understand that the two of you had dinner together last night. Could you tell us where and what time you met and finished?" The woman stood up and paced a bit then sat back down. "I came up for a week-long visit with my daughter. I arrived yesterday mid-afternoon. I met Madelyn about fifteen minutes past eight last night at Le Gourmand on Northwest Market Street. We stayed till about ten, then she said she had to go back to the office and she'd meet me at home in a couple of hours. She never came home, so I phoned the police station. Around noon, an officer appeared at my door with the news that my daughter had been found, but I'd never get to talk with her again." Silent tears fell down the cheeks of the woman, but she made no move to wipe them away. Hailey admired the woman's strength and hoped that when she was as old as this woman, she would look as good and strong as she did. She reached over and patted her knee in a vain attempt to console the her. "I'm sorry for your loss and the pain you are bearing." Hailey stood up and went to the window. Bobby continued questioning the woman, while Hailey slipped out and went in search of an office. Maybe she'd find something that would connect the victim to the other three. She found an office behind the fourth door she tried and slipped inside without a sound. The room was cluttered with ornaments ranging in size from tiny to seven feet tall, she guessed. The little ones didn't hold her attention for long though. The tall statues of angels and saints basically dragged her to them. The craftsmanship in the carvings was remarkable. The faces were so lifelike Hailey had to turn away. She went over to the desk and booted up the computer. In no time at all, she was copying all of the files on to a disc she had brought with her. She shut down the system and left the room as quietly as she had entered. When she slipped back into the parlor, Bobby was just finishing up his questioning. Hailey gave him a thumbs-up and went out to the car. A few minutes later, she watched Bobby exit the house and get in. "That's one tough lady in there." They pulled out of the gates and headed for the station to meet up with Gabe. "What did you get from your tour, Hailey?" She pulled out the disc. "This right here might have something or nothing, other than that, not much except Ms. Groves has an odd collection of orna-ments in her office."

"You mean had. Now the old lady gets them. Why do you suppose the old lady was so ..."

"Emotionless?" Bobby nodded. "My guess is breeding. That family is old money."

"How can you tell?"

"The way the old lady held herself and her demeanor plus that house. A sin-gle woman could not afford that house and everything in it on an assistant law clerk's salary." That, by Hailey's definition, was old money. "Either that or Mob money." She chuckled and slipped the disc back into her pocket. Bobby backed into his spot at the station. Up in the homicide unit, Gabe was sitting at the thinking table with his head down and his hand writing furiously. Hailey went directly to the computer and booted up the disc, Bobby sat across from Gabe, and they started going over their notes. "We talked to the victim's mother, and she said she met up with her daughter for dinner around eight. They stayed at the restaurant for a couple of hours then the daughter said she had to go back to the office so she'd meet her mother at home later. She never came home." Gabe grunted. "Sounds like maybe the office gossip was right. Perhaps she was sleeping with her boss?" Bobby sat back and rolled his shoulders. This case was making him tense. "Well, if she was, I don't think she made the date. I think the killer got to her first." He stood up and went to pour himself some coffee. Gabe had his face scrunched up in thought when Bobby sat back down. "Hell! Maybe she did go back to the office, like she told her mom. Now that I think about it, the stuff I picked up about her from the office, not the gossip, leads me to believe that she did go back to the office. Hailey searched her desk, and she said that it was clean. Everything on or in that desk had a use. I even went over it before I left the building, and the lady was a neat freak."

"Hailey slipped into her home office and copied files from her computer, but I imagine that that office was spotless also." He turned to Hailey. "Was the victim's home office as clean as her office desk?" She shrugged. "It was clut-tered but clean, no dust, everything in its place ... pencils sharpened, pens capped, and paper piled. The room was littered with ornaments and statues of all shapes and sizes, though. She had a love affair with angels and such, I think." She turned back to the computer and began scanning again. Bobby turned back to Gabe. "Any suspects brewing in your list of coworkers?" Gabe rifled through his note-pad. "I've started to compile a list. It's very short. Most everyone had alibis, so we have about ten people who didn't. A couple of them were not at the office today, but I have home addresses and phone numbers. I've checked all alibis so they're clear. My list is short but it has merit." He handed it to Bobby. "Have you checked backgrounds on your list yet?" Gabe shook his head no. "I was about to when you two showed up." Bobby handed back the pad. "Let's do it. Split it in half. I'll take the bottom half." He scribbled down the last five names and numbers and then left the room. Five minutes later, he was back with printouts.

CHAPTER 16

Hailey stood up from the computer and went to pour herself some coffee. "You two working or just pretending?" Bobby and Gabe both gave her a grunt, and she laughed and went back to the computer. All of the files she had scanned so far were nothing but usual home files: accounts, bills, journal entries. Nothing unusual. She hit a few keys, then suddenly a small file popped up with the heading "SECRET". Hailey straightened up and punched a few more keys and opened the file. The screen started to scroll with computer talk which stopped with a prompt to enter the password. "I think I might have found something guys," Hailey threw over her shoulder. Bobby and Gabe went over and stood behind her while she entered the command and opened the file.

* * * *

He awoke with a scream lodged in his throat. His body was drenched with sweat, and his chest was heaving. He stumbled to the bathroom and splashed cold water on his face, trying to level his breathing and bring his eyes to focus. He remembered dreaming he was a little boy running in the dark woods behind his childhood home. Something was chasing him but he couldn't turn to see what it was. He remembered feeling the hard earth under his feet while they pounded down and the pain in his chest with his heavy breaths. There were tears streaming down his cheeks, and then suddenly, he heard a scream from behind. He dropped to his knees and matched the scream with one of his own. With his breathing under control, he moved to his kitchen. His stomach was grumbling with hunger, so he pulled out some ingredients to make some of his mother's French toast. The voices had left him in peace since his last kill, which worried him. When were they going to scream again and for whom? The kill came back to him now. Small parts flashed in his mind like a movie. Shot after shot came back. He saw himself burning her eyes then savagely ripping open her chest. In his mind's eye, he picked up his smallest scalpel and began the careful process of removing her heart without damaging it. He stood up and moved to a back room. In the room stood a tall, narrow fridge.

He went to the fridge and opened it. Inside, there were four hearts, each in their own clear container with their own label. He reached in and pulled out the last one. He studied it then carefully replaced it and closed the fridge door. He headed back to his bedroom and out onto his deck. The sky was clear tonight; for that, he was grateful. He breathed in the cool night air and stared up at the moon. He remembered sleeping outside as a little boy in the backyard. That was before he got sick. There was a faint whisper in the back of his mind. He didn't want to hear it tonight, so he quickly went inside to his bed and grabbed his pills off the night stand. He swallowed two dry and laid down. Closing his eyes, he saw the kill flashe before him. A lone tear escaped. He felt tomorrow was going to be a long day with something deadly to end it.

*   *   *   *

"This looks to be a journal of sorts. Something about her boss and the way he looks at her." Hailey skimmed the rest while Bobby and Gabe read over her shoulder. "Why would she make a separate file for her affair? Why not just add it to her journal?" Gabe asked while he went to pour them all some coffee. Hailey shrugged. "The way she writes about him says she was a little more than in love with him. She writes here that his wife almost caught them a few weekends ago in his town house, and she wishes she had so that he could marry her and leave the 'old bag.'" Bobby grunted and took a swallow of his coffee, wincing at the bitterness. "I think I'll pay a visit to her boss. Sounds like she was on the verge of stalking. Then I'll go and have a chat with the wife, maybe she did know about the affair and that's a prime motive right there." Hailey looked up at Bobby. "You can't tell me that you think this was a revenge murder? I know a woman didn't kill her."

"There's no harm in talking. Besides, the last victim was sloppy, so maybe it was a copycat." He grabbed his jacket and headed out the door knowing full well that this was no copycat. "He feels lost, Gabe. There will be another death, and I think it'll be soon." She shut down the computer and stood up. "How far did you two get on the background checks?" She sat down in the chair Bobby had vacated and shuffled through the printouts. "I didn't get very far, but everyone on my list is looking clean." He went back to reading his printouts while Hailey started at the beginning of Bobby's. The first three on the list were as clean as lawyers could be. The fourth had a few minor charges from his youth but he leads a clean life now. The last person on the list struck Hailey as odd. The earliest known knowledge of, she flipped her gaze over to the list and read the name, a Mr. Edward Mercurial was only about thirty years ago when he joined the firm. He had just popped up out of nowhere it seemed. Hailey knew that wasn't possible, but it was possible that he had a former identity. She picked up the phone and called Ramsey Kage at the FBI headquarters. "Agent Kage."

"Ramsey, it's Hailey. Got a minute?" They exchanged some small talk then she asked him to do a background check on Edward Mercurial and to try and dig up anything and everything pertaining to him before thirty years ago. "I guess I could, but why are you asking me when I know you could find the info just the same if not quicker?" She laughed. "I figured I would do this the proper way and get an official government agent to do the digging. I wouldn't want to break any laws." She heard him chuckle. "I'll get the info for you and download it to your computer. Give me twenty-four hours." They both hung up simultaneously. She was confident Ramsey would dig up something.

CHAPTER 17

Bobby was sitting in one of the most uncomfortable chairs he had ever come across while the woman across from him, who looked like a plastic doll in his opinion, gave him a rundown of how pathetic her husband was. "When I married the bastard, he was the most caring and dashing man. Then about three years ago, he turned into a lying, cheating scumbag. I caught him sleeping with the maid, so I fired her, and then he started sleeping with the new maid, who I might add was only twenty-two!" He just nodded and clucked his tongue while jotting down names, dates, and numbers. The woman was pacing the room now and flapping her arms wildly. Bobby thought to himself, *Why did I think this woman might have had something to do with the latest murder? She is so hysterical right now she wouldn't have been able to do what was done.*

"Well, thanks for your time." He quickly stood. "I'm sorry to have bothered you, and I do hope you have a good evening. I'll see myself out." He left the room with her still ranting and pacing; he wasn't even sure if she'd heard him talk. He walked through the squad door just as Hailey hung up the phone. Glancing over at Gabe, he noticed he was scowling down at the desk. "What's got you, Nexs?" Gabe looked up. "Nothin." He scowled back at the desk. Bobby glanced over at Hailey, she just shrugged. "How'd your chat go with the wife?" He rubbed his hand behind his neck and rolled a chair over. "The lady didn't do it. She was a cracker, that one was. I can understand why the hubby would commit adultery. It sounded like she probably rode his ass a lot."

"I went over your half of this list here, and everyone but the last guy checks out. There's no known identity of this guy before thirty years ago. It's as if he just …" She waved her hand in the air. "… appeared. I called in a favor for a background check; maybe he'll get lucky for us." Bobby read the printout she handed him. "Started at firm at age of twenty-three. Graduated top of his class. Started at the bottom and worked hard, up the lawyerly ladder for the past thirty years. One of the top lawyers in the firm and in line for a partnership." Then came the basics like the address and phone numbers where he could be reached. "It reads like a usual middle-aged man's life." He handed back the printout. "Well, yes, but there's nothing before the firm. All of the other printouts give lifetime information. So ... where the hell is his? I just find it odd, and so should you." She stood up and started pacing. Bobby watched her for a few minutes considering. "You said you called in a favor. Why don't we just wait and see what he pulls up? No sense in jumping to conclusions and assuming. I'm surprised at you Hailey. Why are you so jumpy all of a sudden?" She stopped pacing and stared at the two of them, Gabe, with his gentle brown eyes and unruly dark blond hair, his lumberjack build squeezed into an awful gray wrinkled suit, slumped there in his chair and Bobby, with his marine-style shaved head and small, unreadable gray eyes, sitting straight, always looking like he was going to pounce, in a rich, dark blue suit. He was studying her. How was she supposed to explain to these two that she got the willies from reading that last name on the list? Her time in the Corps, had taught her to trust her instincts and always go with her gut, and her gut was telling her that something was up with this Edward Mercurial. Bobby cleared his throat. "Hailey? What's up, girl?" She refocused on him. "I think we should keep a close eye on this guy. I'm going home, and then I'm going to go stake out his place tonight, gather some information. I'll talk to you guys tomorrow." She gathered her stuff and left. Gabe leaned back in his chair. "Sometimes she scares me. Did you see the way she was studying us? Kinda creeped me out. Want some coffee?" He stood up and went and poured them both some. "I noticed," Bobby said quietly. Why would she be so intent on this guy? Sometimes she scared Bobby too. "Nothing on your end of the list, hey, Gabe?" He reached over and picked up his list. Every name was crossed out with a quick note written beside each one. One would never guess that this writing was done by a man who looked like Gabe Nexs. It was clear and precise, not chicken scratch like Bobby's. "Nah. Everyone checks out." Gabe swiveled in his chair, drinking his coffee while Bobby sat still with his arms on his desk and his hands wrapped around his coffee mug, a scowl carved into his face. They weren't any closer to finding the killer than they were yesterday. Hailey was acting strange. They had four victims in the morgue, and he was pretty sure they were going to find another before this thing ended. He scowled and pulled out the autopsy reports.

*   *   *   *

Hailey glanced up at the window where she knew Bobby and Gabe were sitting. She also knew that right this minute, Bobby was trying to figure out what was "wrong" with her. She smiled and opened her door. The guy was always making her into more than she actually was. She found it sweet. Pulling out onto the freeway, Hailey headed for home and mentally started packing for her stakeout tonight.

Three hours later, Bobby was still in his chair pouring over the autopsy reports. Gabe groaned, stretched, and rubbed his hands over his face. "Gotta go home. Bed and beer are a calling." He threw his jacket on. "Don't pound your head against those files too long, Stein." Bobby grunted and sent him a wave. Just a couple more hours he told himself then he'd go home for a beer and bed.

CHAPTER 18

Sitting in her Range Rover in the dark, Hailey watched the house across the street. It was a two-level brick house with a wrap-around porch. All of the lights were off, but there was a BMW in the drive. She'd been watching the house for a couple of hours now and was getting ready to do a perimeter check of the grounds. She'd brought night-vision goggles, a Beretta with custom-made silencer, a lock-pick, a digital camera, and a wide variety of micro-bugs, a little gift from a friend in high places. She closed up her pack, slipped the Beretta into her holster and the goggles on her head, and then grabbed her small but surprisingly strong flashlight. Popping a piece of peppermint gum into her mouth, she exited her Rover and slinked across the street. Her training took over mind and body. She had tried long and hard to extinguish her life as a Marine but eventually realized that it wasn't the Marine she was trying to extinguish but herself. Her shrink had helped her with some things, and with the others, she had managed on her own.

Crouching in the shadows of the trees behind the house, she slipped the goggles on and scanned the area. With the goggles on, her vision was perfect in the dark. She took two deep breaths, closed her eyes, and tuned all of her senses to her surroundings. She heard a dog bark to the right and a light jazz sound from the left. In the yard, a cat stalked its prey through the grass and the trees swayed, rustling the leaves and making them sound like whispers of the unknown. She crept silently towards the house. Nothing stirred. She heard the night and nothing more. Reaching the door, she pulled out her lock-pick and was in the house in under a minute. Bobby pulled up behind her Rover just as she was slipping inside the house. He shut off his car and climbed out. By the time he reached the driver's side window, he was swearing so badly his ears had started to ring. Calming himself down, he climbed into her passenger seat and decided to wait her out. In his mind, he saw her slinking around the house, melding into the corners and doors. He wasn't sure how long he had been sitting there when suddenly, she was sitting in the driver's seat drinking a cup of coffee. He studied her. She had an ear-piece in her ear and, was chewing something and jotting notes down on a pad. He promised himself he wasn't going to yell. "What the hell do you think you're doing?" She swallowed and turned her head. *He sure looks mad, she thought to herself, but he's trying hard to restrain it.* "My job." She handed him the thermos and pulled out her ear-piece. "Your job? How do you figure breaking and entering is your job?! I could have you arrested!" Hailey smiled and patted his leg. "Your voice is rising, Stein." He sucked in his breath and counted to ten. "What are you doing here anyways?" she asked him. Glaring at her, he growled, "I thought you might want some company. You're supposed to sit and watch on a stakeout, not sneak around like a thief!"

"Why did you hire me?" He stared out the window. "You hired me for my skills and the fact that I can go places you guys can't, get information you guys can't. Now, in order for me to do that, I have certain methods and means to accomplish it." Hailey watched his profile while she gave him her speech. She noticed how the anger smoothed out and the admission set in. Slowly, he faced her again. Everything she said was true. He did hire her for all that she had just told him. "All right. I agree with you, so I'm just going to go home, have a beer, and hit the sack. Good-night, Hailey." He got out and stalked to his car. He flashed his tail-lights when he reached the end of the block and turned left, leaving Hailey in the dark. Smiling to herself, she resumed her recording of her tour of the subject's house. In her mind, it was laid out like a photograph. It was a typical single man's home. Each room on the ground floor she had entered and placed a little something in was furnished easily and sparsely. Upstairs, there were three rooms and a bathroom. Two of the rooms were empty but the room at the end of the hallway was where she had seen the subject. After entering the room low and crawling to the phone, she had placed a bug in the receiver. She then took a picture of the sleeping man and exited the house the same way she had entered. She headed back to the Rover. When she climbed into the seat and saw Bobby snoozing in the passenger seat with that mean scowl of his, she had almost shoved him out of the vehicle, but she had restrained herself and instead began tuning her receiver into the frequency of the bugs she had planted throughout the house. She had just started jotting down her notes when he woke up and started his tirade. Anyway, he was gone now so she sat and watched the house again. *This is a long shot, she thought to herself, but what other leads do we have?* At that moment, an upstairs light came on. She knew it was the master bedroom from her tour before. Then, just as suddenly, the light went out, and about four minutes later, the front door opened and a shadow got into the car in the driveway. She decided to follow the car, so when it pulled around the corner, she started her Rover and followed behind at a safe distance. She glanced at her watch and read the time as 1:00 am. She wondered where the car was going so late in the night. After she had followedfor about twenty minutes, he pulled into a parking lot. She pulled the Rover in several vehicles down from him and watched him enter the pub. Glancing up at the sign as she walked towards the door, she read Trev's Place. She entered and went up to the bar, grabbing a stool at the end in the shadows. Trevor spotted her and brought her a beer which she gladly accepted. "You're not bringing any more bad news, I hope?" Hailey smiled. "No. Just in for a beer. I do have a question for you, though." Hailey swiveled a bit. "See that guy over in the far corner behind me?" Trevor glanced over her shoulder. "I see him."

"Do you recognize him?" Trevor studied the man in question. All he could make out was a dark outline of a man sitting in the corner with a drink in his hands. "He doesn't look familiar, but that doesn't mean he doesn't frequent." He wandered down the bar to refill glasses and clear away those that had been left then made his way back down the bar to her. "I'll ask Courtney if she recognizes him." Trevor wandered over to the other end of the bar just as Courtney came up to gather her orders. Hailey watched him lean in. Courtney shook her head then glanced over her shoulder. When she looked at him again, he pointed down to Hailey. She nodded and grabbed her tray. She deftly served her drinks and with a swish of her hips, walked towards Hailey. "Hey there. The boss tells me you want to know if I recognize the guy in the corner." She hummed and clacked her gum. "I think I might have seen him in here once or twice before, but I can't be sure. I could go get friendly with him if you want." She stood there looking at Hailey, swinging her tray and blowing bubbles with her gum. Hailey shook her head and thanked her for the offer. Courtney shrugged and went back to serving her customers. After finishing her beer and sending a wave to Trevor, Hailey went back out to her Rover and decided to wait and watch for him there.

* * * *

The voices had woken him up again so he came here. He picked the same table as before, but something felt different. The voices were muffled in here, but this time, he kept hearing one distinct voice. It kept telling him to look. For what?" He screamed in his head. The rest of the voices fought for volume, causing his head to start pounding. Tossing back the last of his drink, he noticed how his hands shook. The ice rattling was like loud pings in his ears causing his already pounding head to throb even more incessantly. He dropped the glass on the table and shoved the chair back. It fell to the floor with a thud, and he staggered out of the bar. He felt many hands on him as he bumped into people on his way out the door, but all he saw was a blur. Once outside, he fell to the ground and breathed deeply. The pounding receded, and the voices were once again talking at a mumble. After a few minutes, he stood up. They were telling him to find the girl who knew. He shook his head. He didn't want anymore blood on his hands. The voices got louder with every denial he made. He got into his car and, pounded the wheel with his fists so hard he cracked his flesh. The voices kept up at a steady buzz in his head. He started the car and drove out of the parking lot heading anywhere.

*   *   *   *

Hailey watched him fall out the door onto his hands and knees. She watched as he shook violently, Then, just as suddenly as he started shaking, he stopped. The man in the trench coat stood up, and she watched as he dusted himself off and started talking to himself. She rolled down her window, but he was talking too quietly for her to hear. He then walked to his car. About ten minutes later, she watched as his car went by out of the parking lot. She started up her Rover and pulled out to follow him.

CHAPTER 19

Bobby awoke to the sharp shrill of his alarm at five after six the next morning. He rolled out of bed and wandered into the bathroom. In his kitchen, the coffee-maker automatically dripped and his parrot, Jim, started to whistle. Twenty minutes later, he was in his kitchen straddling a chair while drinking his morning cup and scanning the paper. His hip started to vibrate. The beeper screen showed Gabe's number, so he reached over to the phone and speed-dialed. "Morning'. What's up?" On the other end, he heard Gabe cough then a rustle. "Sorry, mornin'. Catch a ride in with you? Grab some breakfast and recap?"

"Sure. I'll be there in fifteen." Bobby hung up the phone, finished his coffee, fed Jim, and left the house. He pulled into Gabe's driveway eighteen minutes later and honked his horn. Slamming the car door, Gabe grinned at Bobby. "After breakfast, let's go by the morgue. I wanna talk to the doc some more." An hour later, they had arrived at the morgue. A cute little brunette informed them that Doctor Jackson was unavailable at the moment, but if they wanted to wait, she didn't think he'd be much longer than twenty minutes. She offered them coffee then went back to her work. Fifteen minutes later, she told them that they could go in. They walked into Rye's office where he was going over a file with the assistant they had seen the last few times they were there. Rye looked up, saw them standing at his door, and waved them in. "I'll just be a few more minutes. Have a seat."

They each grabbed a chair and watched while Rye pointed out a few mis-takes in the file he was looking through. The assistant nodded then left the office with a curt nod towards the detectives. "It's been a few days since we last saw each other. What can I do for you?" Bobby looked at Gabe. This was his show so he was letting him do all the talking. Gabe cleared his throat. "I'd like to go over the bodies again." Rye nodded. "Okay, but we'll have to use the files." He pulled out five red files from a drawer. "Is there anything in particular you're looking for?" Gabe shrugged his shoulders. "I'm actually not too sure. I just think we should go over them again." Rye nodded then handed them each a file. Bobby opened the file in front of him. It was the autopsy of the first victim, Shelia Voice. He read through it then tossed it and picked up the fifth file lying on the doctor's desk. *Maybe this last victim will tell me something the first four haven't, he thought to himself.* Opening it, he read the name, Madelyn Groves. He scanned the report and then flipped to Rye's notes.

'*Victim's' skin shows little signs of any form of abuse. There are two small circular bruises, which were determined to have been inflicted with a small metal clamp with an electrical current running through, located on each temporalis muscle. Wrists and ankles show signs of prolonged application of tight ligatures. There is a linear zone extending circularly around each ankle and wrist. The zone contains very few hairs or hair follicles, and there were trace amounts of a dark fiber embedded in the lesions which was tested to be a brand of a navy-colored nylon. The electric shock was received shortly before death. The heart was removed through a savagely ripped chest opening. The extraction of the heart, however, was cleanly done with the vital arteries cut. The circulatory system shows nearly invisible signs of disruption with cells. All other organs are intact. A small incision was found in the inner thigh. Embedded in the incision was a note written in Latin. As with each victim, the note was obscure. The only difference with this victim from the other four was the fact that she was found partially clothed and her face was clean of all beatings except for the eyes. The eyes were burnt, prior to death, with a thin iron rod. Small traces of iron were found in the eye cavity along with inflammation of surrounding tissue.*'

Bobby flipped through the file and found a copy of the translated note. Then he rifled through the other four files and pulled out the copies of the notes and laid them out in order of death on the floor in front of him. He then proceeded to read them.

"*Gathering abundance brings peace of mind. I will collect those that prove to be of pure heart to cleanse myself of all impurities.*"

"*One is done: two will be through. Pure of heart is to be true.*"

"*A snake in the grass before light, to disgust by God's grace.*"

"*Out of nothing, nothing comes. At my own risk, an evil in itself. He who is silent gives consent.*"

"*The just is blessed, but the name of the wicked shall rot.*"

Gabe put down his file and looked over the notes as well. "This guy is a nut job." Bobby nodded. "A well-educated nut job. He wrote these all in Latin, and I think they all have references to God or religious aspects. Like this first note …" He got out of his chair and pointed down to the note. "… could imply that he killed her to cleanse himself of his sins and to release her from her torment.

The second as well could refer to the missing hearts. Hailey suggested that the killer shows childish behavior, and he's regressing. Then there's the third note." He paced to the window and back. "Talking about 'a snake in the grass' which I assume is a sort of symbol about himself stalking his prey. 'To disgust by God's grace' probably refers to why he killed his victim. He's saying she sinned." He looked up at Gabe to make sure he was understanding him and noticed that he had Rye's attention as well. "The fourth note confuses me a little. It's almost like he doesn't even know what he's trying to say. "'Out of nothing, comes nothing.'" Could mean that his reason for killing is obscured in his mind. Then he goes on to talk about an evil in itself which probably means him. The fifth note is an excerpt from the Old Testament. After reading these, it only seems possible that what Hailey suggested about childish behavior is correct, and he more than likely is very well educated and probably spent some if not all of his time in a mental hospital. I'm going on my gut, but I'd bet a Catholic one."

CHAPTER 20

He stopped pacing and sat down again. Gabe pulled out one of his cigars and began to stroke it between his fingers. Rye got up and poured himself some coffee then sat back down again. In mid-stroke, Gabe stopped and looked at the doctor. "You only found one flower in place of the heart right?" He nodded. "The first victim." He shuffled around the files and pulled out Sheila Voice's. "In place of the heart was a large white lily which I sent to the lab to test. Turns out that the flower was synthetically made." Gabe shifted in his seat. "But you found nothing else in the other bodies. Why do you think he only left something in one body but not the rest?" All three of them sat there when Bobby stood up again. "I don't think there is a reason." Standing in front of the window, Bobby asked Gabe, "Have you heard from Hailey today?" He watched an old street lady pushing a buggy laden with her treasures, which looked like trash to Bobby, across the street. "Haven't seen or heard from her since last night." Gabe glanced at Rye who shook his head no. "Neither of us has heard from her. What's brewing in that head, Stein?" Bobby rolled his shoulders. His gut was starting to churn, and he usually took that as trouble, but it was just a nibble right now, so he pulled an antacid out of his pocket and went back to his chair. "Haven't heard from her is all." Rye's phone suddenly let off a low beep followed by a soft voice informing him that the "Senelly case" was downstairs then a low click. Rye gathered the files and put them away, and then the three of them left his office.

Back on the road, Bobby and Gabe headed to the precinct. As he sat there, Gabe couldn't help but study Bobby. He noticed that Bobby was grinding his jaw, and he was glaring on and off. He'd known Bobby long enough to know that something was burning in his mind but he also knew better than to ask what it was. A few minutes later, Bobby's cell phone shrilled. He answered with a grunt then abruptly growled, "Where are you?" He slapped his phone shut then made a U-turn. All Gabe heard was a blast of horns, then they were turning the corner. "Where are we going, and is it really necessary to drive like a maniac?" Bobby growled at him and kept driving.

*   *   *   *

Hailey hung up her phone then swiveled to look out her deck window. Bobby had sounded furious on the phone just like she knew he would be. She knew why he was mad, but he'd calm down once she told him what she had dug up, she was sure. She poured herself some tea then reread the file Ramsey had sent her. From what she could tell, he hadn't found much on Edward Mercurial. He was born Curtis Treckle on February 6, 1949. He was orphaned at a young age after being found by police sleeping with his murdered parents. He was sent to an orphanage for only a few weeks, and then he was transferred to a Catholic mental institution in Europe. It didn't say who paid for the transfer. He spent his life there till he was eighteen and was treated for acute schizophrenic episodes along with denial and elective mutism. He then dropped out of existence till he was twenty-four where he popped up as Edward Mercurial and enrolled in Harvard Law School. He graduated cum laude and was employed by one of the top five law firms in Seattle where he steadily climbed the ranks.

That was everything Ramsey had sent her, which was more than she had had. Reading it made her quite sure that they had the right man, and she hoped Bobby and Gabe would see it that way also. She sat back and waited for the guys to show up going over everything in her mind. It was only last night that they had nothing really to go on, and now she was sure they had the killer. The only thing to do now was to collect more evidence, only she wasn't too sure on how to go about that at this point in time. Just then, she heard her door slam, and two seconds later, Bobby stormed in with a mean scowl etched into his face and Gabe hot on his trail, only not armed with a scowl but with a sneaky grin instead.

CHAPTER 21

"What am I doing on the floor?" He awoke on his living room floor around noon the next day. He remembered waking up in the night because of the headache then going for a drink at that pub where she worked. He went to his kitchen for a glass of water. He remembered that the voices were getting louder and his hands were shaking so badly that he couldn't hold his drink anymore so he left the pub. He had driven aimlessly for a long time before he noticed that there was a dark-colored sedan following him. Then he remembered purposely driving around for about two more hours and stopping at a corner store. When he exited the store, the sedan wasn't anywhere he could see, so he got into his car and drove home.

Once he parked, he remembered sitting in his car looking in every shadow before he went to the door. Then he was awake on his living room floor, and the clock told him it was noon. Upstairs in his bedroom, Edward stripped down and walked naked to the shower. He noticed that today was the first day he'd felt great in two months. He heard not a peep of the voices, not even a slight pounding in his skull. He sang quietly to himself while he scrubbed himself raw. After drying himself off, he hung the towel up then went back to his room and opened his closet doors. He stood in front of the open doors for a few minutes and absently stroked himself. He started to walk into the closet, but suddenly, he turned and walked to the bed where he lay down on his back. His left hand was still stroking while his right hand reached for the bedside table drawer. He suddenly jerked in pain, and a red haze then blackness clouded his mind. A few minutes later, he awoke to find his hands covered in blood and the tip of his penis bleeding. He looked down beside himself to find the scalpel that had done the damage, and he quickly looked around for his assailant before he realized that he was the only one there. Grabbing the closest thing to him, which happened to be the shirt he'd worn the night before, he applied pressure to his wound. He returned to the bathroom and started to clean up, stitching up what he could and bandaging it once he was done. He took four more pain killers than he normally took for his headaches and went back into his room to get dressed. His bed was a bloody mess, so he bundled up his top blanket and set it close to his door. He'd burn it later tonight. He got dressed *then went to his office. Since he was feeling great, he decided to get some work done so he wouldn't be so far behind when he went back to the office. Ten minutes later, he was shaking uncontrollably and sweating profusely, lying on the floor next to his chair.*

* * * *

"Have a seat, boys." She gave a hard look at Bobby telling him to keep his mouth shut. She was amazed when he actually sat down without saying a word. She stood up and poured coffee for them and tea for herself then sat back down and handed them each a copy of the file Ramsey had sent her. She sipped her tea while watching as they read it. Bobby finished his copy first and slowly strangled it as he glared at her desk. Hailey didn't say a word until Gabe set his copy down a few minutes later. "He's our killer." Bobby looked at her, but Gabe spoke first. "Why do you think he's the killer when we have nothing even remotely close to tying him to any one of the victims?" Hailey sat there watching Bobby. "Madelyn Groves, the latest victim, was his secretary, and he fits the profile on the killer. He was never interviewed. He's the only one on that list from the firm that hasn't been questioned." Bobby stood up and started pacing. He couldn't contain his anger any longer, but he promised himself he would keep his voice even. "You should have checked in sooner. You should have contacted me this morning." Hailey smiled. "Yes, Daddy, and I'll tell that boy to stop following me home too." Her comment made him stop. "Look …" She stood up. "I run my business my way. You hired me. Back-off and let me do my job, Stein, and if you can't handle that, then maybe I should quit." She poured some more tea for herself and coffee for Gabe but none for Bobby since he had yet to touch his. "This suspect, Edward Mercurial, is our killer, and I plan on stopping him, hopefully before he kills again, and I know you'd rather I do it with you than without, so stop being pissy and let's start thinking how we're going to catch him." He was still tense when he sat back down, but he could feel his temper slowly fading out. He couldn't help getting pissed off at her because he loved, her but he would never tell her so. In the end, it did him no good to argue with her anyways because she was usually right and that pissed him off even more. He counted down from twenty then spoke. "Okay. So he's our killer. Fine. We need to set a trap then, since we have nothing pinning him to all the murders. First, Gabe and I will interview him. I'll get my own perspective, then we'll talk about the next step." She opened a drawer in her desk and pulled out a thin envelope which she handed to Bobby. "This is a picture of the suspect. When you interview him, you can compare and see if it's the same guy."

Twenty minutes later, the guys left and Hailey turned to her computer. She opened her email and sent Ramsey a quick thank-you for all his help and promised they'd get together soon and catch up. She then rinsed out the mugs and went out on her deck. She planned better outside than in, and she had to figure out a way to catch Edward before he killed again. She popped back into her office for a moment then returned with what looked like a Walkman and sat down. She fiddled with the dial for a few minutes then slipped the headphones on. She heard silence for a few minutes then rustling. It took her a few minutes to realize it was paper being shuffled. Then there was a cough, followed by more rustling and the chink of a glass being knocked against something. She smiled to herself knowing that the bugs she laid were in working order, and she giggled to herself knowing what Bobby's reaction would be if he knew what she was doing this very moment. She listened for awhile longer then got up to make herself something to eat. She returned in time to hear his door-bell chime and the soft swoosh of a wheeled chair being rolled along carpet.

CHAPTER 22

He was in the middle of reading a brief when he heard the door-bell chime. He threw back the rest of his drink, deciding whether to answer or ignore the door. He decided to answer it. He glanced at himself in the mirror on his way to the door and stopped dead in his tracks. Observing himself, he noticed the paleness of his skin and his bloodshot eyes staring back at him. Suddenly, he heard the voices again, only they were very muffled. They were telling him to ignore the door, but instead, he ignored them. He opened the door to find two men standing on his porch both in wrinkled suits. They introduced themselves as detectives and asked if they could have a few words with him. He hesitated only a minute, then stepped back and let them enter. The three of them stood in his foyer uncomfortably until he led them into his sitting room. "How can I help you, gentlemen?" he asked while he poured himself a drink. He offered them nothing and sat back down in a huge leather chair opposite them and waited for a response. Gabe stood up and went to stand by the window, pulling out a cigar. Bobby informed Mr. Mercurial that they were there in regards to the death of his secretary, Madelyn Groves. He nodded his head and took a drink noticing that even though the voices were driving him to distraction, his hands were steady. "I'm not sure how I can help you with that, Detective. I left work early that day, and she was fine when I left."

"I understand, sir, but it's just routine that we question everyone who had contact with her and you're the last on our list. To be honest, we've had a hell of a time trying to contact you." Bobby noticed his blood-shot eyes and how they were darting back and forth between himself and Gabe over by the window. There were little signs of nervousness in the man sitting across from him even though he could detect no shaking in his hands. He had the feeling that the man was distracted. He went about asking the usual questions, which he answered with the common responses. *Edward wanted the men to leave. The one asking him questions was studying him intently while the other one was wandering around the room. They were making him nervous, and the voices were getting louder. Abruptly, interrupting Bobby in mid-question, he stood up. "Excuse me." He fled the room with as much grace as he could and slipped into the bathroom. He grasped the counter and squeezed his eyes shut tight. The voices were yelling now, causing his head to pound like a hundred jackhammers thumping into the ground. He opened his eyes and shivered at the reflection in the mirror. Releasing the counter, he opened the medicine cabinet and pulled out a bottle of aspirin. He shook out ten tablets and swallowed them dry. He knew they wouldn't do much, but he prayed they would at least dim the voices enough so he could make it through the rest of the questions he knew the detectives wanted to ask him. After splashing cold water on his face, he took several deep breaths, composing himself.*

Gabe was scanning the shelves. "Should we leave soon?" he asked. "I have a couple more questions for him, then we will."

"He's pretty nervous, Stein. I have a feeling Hailey might be on to something here." Just then, Edward suddenly stumbled back into the room right in the middle of Gabe's statement. Gabe looked over at Bobby who shrugged his shoulders.

"Sorry, Detectives. I haven't been feeling very well the last few weeks." He took *his seat again and picked up his drink, swallowing the last of the amber liquid. The room was silent except for the clinking of the ice in the glass as he set it back on the table.* Bobby cleared his throat and flipped through his note-pad. "Just a couple more questions, sir, then we'll leave. How long had Ms. Groves worked for you?" *Edward rubbed his hands on his legs. "About three years, I guess. She was good at her job. I valued her help."* Bobby nodded, and Gabe moved over to the door. "Do you know of anyone who would want to hurt her? Any enemies that you knew of?" Bobby studied his face. He appeared calm, but his eyes were wild, and Bobby felt the hairs on his neck stand on end. Edward just shook his head no. He showed them to the door, but when Bobby held out his hand, Edward just shut the door.

They sat in the car for a few minutes watching the house. "What do you think?" Gabe lit the cigar that he had been holding since they started questioning Mr. Edward Mercurial. Bobby started the car and pulled out onto the road. "I think we had better keep a close eye on Edward Mercurial. Something is going on with him. It looks like Hailey was right." He pulled out the photo she had given him and handed it over to Gabe. The face on the photo was the same as the face they had just questioned.

*   *   *   *

He was sitting on the floor, propped up by the door. Once the detectives had left, his legs had given out on him, and two hours later, he was still sitting in the exact same spot. His head was cradled in his hands and the voices were rampant. He struggled to stand up and staggered up the stairs. The voices were screaming, and he could hear himself sobbing while he tried to pop the top on his pills. Suddenly, the top came off, and the pills spilled everywhere. He dropped to his knees, gathering up four and swallowing them dry, then he fell back onto the floor and closed his eyes. He knew the pills would take a few moments to dim the voices in his head, but he couldn't mistake what they were telling him to do. He struggled to stand up and stumbled into bed. He'd have a nap then do what he ha to Only this time, he'd make sure it was his last.

*   *   *   *

The guys arrived back at Hailey's to find her lounging out on her deck. Her eyes were closed, but Bobby knew she wasn't asleep, so they both pulled up chairs, Gabe lit up another cigar. Bobby just stared at Hailey until she opened her eyes.

CHAPTER 23

Feeling his eyes on her, she decided to keep her eyes closed but removed the headphones. "How'd it go?"

She knew very well how it had gone, but neither one of the detectives knew that, so she decided to let him tell her, then she'd let them hear the tape. "Mr. Edward Mercurial is definitely our closest suspect. He was extremely nervous, but he hid it well. I sent a car over to keep watch on him. He'll call me if anything happens. In the meantime, we figured we'd come back here and hopefully connect him to the other victims. Any ideas?" Gabe stubbed out his cigar and went inside for some coffee. Hailey handed him her listening device. She motioned for him to put it on and to push play. She watched his face go from calm to hostile and braced herself for his blow-up. He calmly set the Walkman look-a-like down, pulled out a smoke, lit it, and then took a few drags. He looked over at Hailey. He knew she was waiting for him to blow up at her, but he wasn't going to. He wasn't even going to mention the tape he had just listened to. Gabe returned and stopped in his tracks. He could feel the tension emanating from Bobby, but he just wasn't too sure what had caused it. He glanced at Hailey, and from her expression, he guessed she had, of course, caused the tension. He decided to give the coffee he had just poured to Bobby and went back inside to pour himself another cup. Bobby took a sip then set it down on the table. "Do you have any idea about the situation that you just put me in?" She watched him, surprised that that was all he had to say. She cleared her throat. "Yes, but I figured you'd want to hear it. I know you can't use it, but my point was to let you know that I will find something with it. I placed them around his house, and I'm sure he'll let something slip." He took a few more swallows of coffee. "Why do you think he'll let something slip? He's working alone." She shrugged. "He talks to himself. I'm pretty sure he's got acute schizophrenia. He has to be the boy from the file, the one who was found with his dead mother. He's a classic case of multiple personality as well, only his fractionated personalities are in his head." Bobby stood up and leaned on the railing. "I know this guy is messed up, but how do you know that that is his problem? Maybe he's just psychotic."

He flicked his cigarette over the rail and turned around. He looked at Gabe, who had been silent since they arrived. "Anything you want to say, Nexs?" Gabe took a drink of his coffee, watching him over the edge. "I tend to agree with Hailey. I watched him while you asked the questions. Something was going on in that head of his. Remember when he practically ran out of the room, right in the middle of your question? He was gone about five minutes, and when he returned, he was some-what calmer except his eyes were wild. I know you noticed." Bobby nodded. Just then, Hailey's office phone rang. Bobby finished his coffee and sat back down. "How are we going to tie him to the other murders, Nexs?" Gabe looked down at the table. "I think we're going to have to trap him. Let him know we're watching. If Hailey's right, and I think she is, then he's close to cracking, so we'll just push him a little." Hailey returned to her chair. "I heard what you suggested, and I'm all for it. The only thing is, we'll need bait … and that'll be me." Both the detectives looked at her. "Don't even bother trying to dissuade me. I'm your only choice. I know the risks, and I want to catch this bastard just as much as the two of you."

"How are you going to make him take you?" Gabe asked while Bobby nodded in agreement. She leaned back in her chair. "I'm not sure, but I'll figure something out. You two just get pushing. I'll keep tabs on your progress, but don't tell Jeremy 'cause you know he'll cancel our plans, and it's the only way to stop this guy." Bobby rubbed the back of his neck. "I'll just tell him what he wants to hear, but you had better not get yourself killed!" They all laughed at that one, but there was an undertone of fear in the air, and it sent chills down her back. They left shortly after, and she started planning her trap.

*   *   *   *

His dreams were covered in blood and women. He thrashed around on his bed, sweating so much his sheets were soaked, but still, he didn't awake. He clawed and scraped his way through a hall of bodies and blood. He felt he was being hunted, and his voices had become faces, yelling and screaming at him to run far and fast, but they were blinding him, causing him to trip and fall over the bodies. Each time he fell, he gagged from the smell and feel of blood covering him from head to toe. He felt the hunter getting closer, and his legs were getting heavier. The dead women at his feet were pulling at him, trying to drag him down. He rounded a corner, and just as the hunter was reaching for him, he awoke with a scream lodged in his throat. His clothes were drenched in his sweat, so he stripped and lay back down on the bed. He could feel his heart racing and his head pounding. The dream was getting hazy, but the feeling of being hunted was still with him. He got up and walked over to the window. He saw a car parked on the street, but he couldn't tell if it was occupied. He continued scanning the street, but his eyes kept going back to the car. The voices were ringing in his head, telling him to prepare for the final kill. Once she was dead, he would be free, and they'd never find him. He backed away from the window, lowering himself back onto the bed. Cradling his head in his hands, he let the tears run down his cheeks. Taking a deep breath, he wiped his face and went to his closet. He had plans to make and a woman to find, but first, he had to eat. After he dressed, he swallowed a few pills to quiet the voices and went downstairs.

*   *   *   *

Gabe and Bobby sat in their car and watched the house. They had both watched as the suspect scanned the street from the upstairs window. They continued to watch as he stood there and stared at their car. They hoped the first step in baiting their suspect had been taken.

CHAPTER 24

Hailey, meanwhile, was sitting at the pub where she had followed Edward a few nights ago. She had paged the detectives and let them in on her first phase. Sitting in a seat covered in shadow not far from the one he had sat in, she watched and waited. Gabe had told her that there had been movement in the suspect's house, so she hoped that at some point, he would show up here. Somehow, she had to make him want her, make him talk to her about the women. She took a drink of her beer. The pub was steady, and she had much to amuse her. There was a group of young guys across the floor who had been hooting and hollering when she had arrived but were now together in song, arm in arm, swaying while they slurred out the lyrics to "Brown Eyed Girl." It made her smile when she looked to the right at a table that was surrounded by four middle-aged women laughing so loudly that the table to their left was staring at them. They, of course, were oblivious.

Up at the bar, Trevor was pouring, sliding, and wiping all at once while maintaining an argument with an old man about some basketball game. Courtney was sashaying her way through tables carrying a tray loaded with drinks in all colors, sizes, and shapes. There were people in couples on the dance floor with other couples spread out everywhere. She even noticed a few loan drinkers like herself dispersed amongst the crowd.

Hailey tossed back the last of her beer and walked up to the bar, placing the bottle in front of herself. She glanced to the door when a blast of cool air hit her. Her senses immediately intensified as she watched Edward Mercurial slink to a back corner table not far from where she had just been sitting. Her muscles had tensed, her skin had flushed, and the hair on the back of her neck had risen as she watched his sneaky entry. No one else had glanced at the door when he had entered, but Hailey had noticed every inch of him from the moment the pub door had closed behind him. She slowly turned around again and found herself looking at Trevor's grinning face. "Another beer?" He waved it in front of her. "Sure." She gave him a smile and then looked down at the bar. She had to collect herself. She took five deep breaths and closed her eyes. When she opened them again, she was calm and her eyes were clear.

He didn't want to come here, but the voices had screamed that she would be here. "The just is blessed, but the name of the wicked shall rot." It was his mantra playing over and over inside his head. He sat with his back to the wall and waited as the blond barmaid slowly made her way to him. He hated her and wished it was she the voices wanted, but they screamed louder when he thought about killing her. He began his search and without moving his head, roamed through the crowd. Everything and everybody was a haze. Colors and actions melded together into a kind of exotic dance that made him feel tense. He proceeded to search the pub, waiting for the one who would become his savior, the one who would end his pain and give him peace. His lips curled into a smile at the thought of his freedom. His eyes reach the bar and passed over about eight men until they fell on the back of a dirty-blond head. As if in slow motion, the head started to turn and he was struck with how gorgeous she seemed to be. The voices went dim, and it was as if they were the only two people in the room.

She sat facing him while he stared back at her. She had felt him the moment his eyes had fallen on her, and it took everything she had to turn slowly around and meet his gaze. She studied his face as his eyes stayed on hers. She couldn't help thinking how attractive he was for an older man. His hair was salt-and-pepper with a close, clean cut, and his facial features were amazingly soft looking. Hailey, unfortunately, knew that this man was a killer, and it was up to her to prove it. She intended to do so. Grabbing her beer, she placed a slightly shy smile on her face and slowly walked over to his table.

CHAPTER 25

He watched as she slowly made her way to him. Everything was still in a haze, except her. She looked like she was an angel sent from God to destroy him, but he wasn't afraid. He was almost euphoric, and that made him feel so quiet.

She was calm. Giving him a smile, she sat down in the chair he pulled out for her. She was sure that he had no idea that it was he who had pulled out the chair, but that didn't matter, she told herself as she looked into his eyes. They were so dark she was sure they were black. She read love, violence, death, and peace in them.

He couldn't talk. The voices were silent, and he smiled. She just sat there and stared at him. It made him uncomfortable, so he took a drink, and as he did, she smiled and lifted hers to her lips. He swallowed, cleared his throat, and smiled back at her. "My name's Edward." He held out his hand.

Hailey looked down at his hand. She watched as her hand slipped into his, and all she could think was that these hands had mutilated four innocent women, and here she was sitting across from the son of a bitch. She quickly pulled her hand back but not so quickly that he would notice. Edward sat across the table just watching her, and it was starting to bother her.

* * * *

Outside the pub, across the street, the detectives were seated in their car waiting. "How long has he been in there?" Gabe asked as he let out a huge yawn. He wished he could go in and have a beer himself, but he couldn't so he took another swallow of his cold coffee and pretended it was a nice cold beer. "A couple hours now. Hailey must be talking to him or something." They both watched as a man and a woman emerged, draped all over each other. They kissed, then the man led her down the street where they rounded a corner and were gone. Bobby yawned. "I'm gonna stretch my legs." He opened the door and stepped outside. Gabe joined him. "What if he doesn't leave with her?" He leaned on the roof of the car while Bobby twisted his arms behind him and rolled his neck. "He will. Hailey'll make sure he does. Besides, if he doesn't take her today, then there's always tomorrow." They both got back into the car.

*   *   *   *

The waitress had brought another beer to Hailey. She still sat across from Edward who was still just staring at her. "Do you come here often?" she asked. He just sat there smiling at her. She made a move to rise, but his hand clasped hers holding her there. *"Don't be coy. You're not leaving."* She looked at him. "Perhaps you'd like to come with me." She gave him a shy smile again, and he smiled back. The voices were starting up again, telling him to take her. He released her hand, tossed back the rest of his drink, and stood. *"No. You're coming with me."* He grabbed her hand and led her to the door.

His grip felt like a vise around her upper arm. He pulled her close, and she could smell his sweat and hear his quite mumbles. She was pretty sure that he did not even realize he was mumbling or that it was in Latin. She couldn't quite distinguish what he was saying, but she figured it didn't matter. If everything goes according to plan, this will be over soon, she thought to herself. He shoved her out the door. Stumbling, she glanced back at him and was shortly stunned in the transformation of his face and demeanor. In the short time it took for them to walk out of the pub, he had turned aggressive, and his face held a dead, cold stare. His eyes were so dark she could almost feel her life being sucked into them. A chill raced up her spine, and her heart went from a mellow hammer to an incessant one. She could feel the panic rising and couldn't help but think that this was how his other victims would have felt if he had abducted them awake. She looked down at her hands and saw that they were shaking. She balled them into fists and took three deep breaths to calm her self down. She had to gain control or this trap would spring on her.

*   *   *   *

Gabe was snoring quietly with his arms folded across his chest, when Hailey practically fell out the entrance to the pub. Bobby gave his leg a hard swat that brought him awake with his gun drawn and his eyes bleary. "Jesus! Watch where you swing that thing!" Bobby yelled. Gabe shook his head. "Fuck you, man! You're the one who hit me." He holstered his weapon and took a drink of the coffee Bobby handed him. As he was lifting the cup, he saw Hailey standing in the parking lot with their suspect not two feet behind her. "How long she been there?"

"A couple minutes. He shoved her out the door, then she just stood there." They watched as Edward placed his hand on her back and shoved her a little. Hailey and the killer got into a BMW and left the parking lot. Bobby started the car, pulled out about four cars behind, and began following them.

An hour later, they were still driving. "What the *hell,* is this guy doing?" Bobby turned and looked at Gabe, who shrugged his shoulders. "Maybe he knows we're following." Bobby shook his head no. "How could he? I can barely see the ass end of his car." He punched the steering wheel. "He's pulling over. Pass him, then we'll go around and park behind them." They drove past and out of the corner of his eye, Gabe could see Hailey in the passenger seat. They circled the block and parked three cars behind. Gabe got out of the car and walked back to the trunk. He popped it open and watched over the lid as Hailey was led into a store. Inside the car, Bobby was checking over his gun. Glancing in the rear-view mirror, he saw Gabe reach into the trunk then close the lid. Two seconds later, he was sitting beside him again only this time, Gabe had a shotgun between his legs. Three minutes later, Hailey and Edward emerged from the store and got back in the BMW.

*   *   *   *

He shoved her into his car, and she felt a sharp stab of fear. She repressed it and calmly sat, in spite of the hand on her back. He shut the door quietly, then went around and sat behind the wheel. *"We're going for a drive."* He said it without any emotion, and Hailey was fascinated by the complete change he had undergone in less than ten minutes. The car started smoothly, and they glided out of the parking lot. She glanced in the side mirror and watched as Bobby and Gabe pulled out behind them.

Studying him while he drove, Hailey watched as he had an argument with himself. She couldn't understand anything he mumbled, then suddenly, they stopped in front of ... she couldn't believe it, a curiosity shop.

He dragged her around the store for a few minutes where he continued to mumble to himself and perspire. He shoved her back into the car and pulled away from the curb, cutting off traffic behind them. She watched as the honking of horns caused him to wince, as if in pain, but he continued to drive. They drove everywhere and nowhere with him constantly mumbling to himself and occasionally glancing in her direction. She caught a glimpse of the detectives behind them and then slowly checked her hidden weapon. The next thing she knew, they were pulling into his driveway. He cut off the engine then came around to her side and dragged her up to the house.

Chapter 26

After another half-hour of driving, they watched as the BMW pulled into Edward's driveway and Hailey was led inside the house. Both detectives exchanged a look, then Gabe got out of the car and ran to the house while Bobby got on the radio to dispatch. "Possible murder suspect. Request backup, use silent approach." The chief got on the line and started yelling, but Bobby was already out of the car and following Gabe's lead.

* * * *

Inside his kitchen, Hailey was shoved violently down into a dark hole. She managed to land without damage and pushed herself up into a squat. Above her, he slammed the trap door shut, and she was plunged into darkness. Waiting till her eyes adjusted, she lifted her right pant leg and pulled out a penlight she had stashed in her sock, then raised her left pant leg and pulled out her .38-auto. Clicking on the light she slowly began to search the room.

* * * *

Outside the house, Bobby met up with Gabe in the shadows. "Backup?" Gabe whispered over his shoulder. "On the way, in silent mode. ETA twenty minutes," Bobby whispered back. They crept along the house to the back. Gabe peered into the kitchen window. Inside, he spotted Edward sitting at the table with his back facing the window. Beyond the kitchen, the house appeared dark.

* * * *

He sat in his kitchen chair and stared down at the trap-door. Am I really going to kill her? he asked himself. The voices were all that answered. He stood up and went into the adjoining room only to return a few seconds later. He sat back down and began tearing up a dark cloth. The voices were screaming inside his head, but he had succumbed to the pain and no longer cared. He knew this would be the last. This one was different. She had come willingly, and that in itself was proof enough for him that what he had done was meant for him, and now his peace would come. The angel in his web was about to die, and with her death would come his absolution.

*   *   *   *

Gabe watched as he rose from the chair and walked into the dark only to return with what looked like a dark fabric of some kind. He watched as Edward began to tear the fabric into strips. He lowered his head to whisper at Bobby, "He's tearing up fabric. I can't see Hailey, and the rest of the house looks dark." Bobby scowled and raised his head to peer in. He saw the suspect sitting at the table, doing exactly what his partner had said. Suddenly, Edward stood up, and Bobby watched as he bent over and lifted up what looked like a piece of the kitchen floor.

*   *   *   *

Directly in front of Hailey was a large metal door. She listened for a few minutes above her head for some sounds of advancement but heard none, so she proceeded towards the door. There was no lock on it, which was expected, she thought, considering no one was supposed to be able to just walk right in. It made no sound as she pulled it open. She slipped her gun into the back of her pants and entered the room. She was astonished at what she had walked into. It was basically an examination room in a morgue. She wandered around poking into drawers and cupboards and finally came up to the fridge. She opened it up and gasped at what she saw inside. There in front of her were all four of the dead girls' hearts. She shut the door. It was time for her to bring him down. She found a spot to sit in and waited for him to come to her.

*   *   *   *

The voices told him it was time. He smiled and stood up. This one was going to be simple not like the rest. An angel of absolution was awaiting him, and he didn't want to be late. He gathered up the strips of cloth and unlatched the trap-door. The voices dimmed as he started down the steps.

*   *   *   *

Bobby watched as Edward slowly descended into the kitchen floor. Once he couldn't spot his head anymore, he motioned for Gabe to go to the door. They flanked it and Bobby twisted the knob. He went in low with Gabe on his heels. Moving further into the kitchen, they found where Edward had disappeared.

Chapter 27

She was sitting on the stool when he walked into the room. *"There you are, my angel. You found my play-room. Are you ready to grant me absolution?"* She watched as he smiled at her and wandered over to the table with the sink attached to it. He laid down some strips of fabric then walked over to the fridge and opened it. *"These hearts are pure now. I extracted them from their impure souls. My voices help me to find the ones who need release, but you're different. Oh, they told me about you, but in a way, you found me."* He turned and looked at her. He had one of the hearts in his hands. Hailey didn't say anything. She wanted him to talk. She wanted him to explain to her why he did it. He faced the open fridge again. *"You have light inside you. I must help let it out. It's my absolution, my release from this hell they placed me in."* He closed the fridge and walked over to a cupboard. Switching on a small stereo, he pulled out the iron rod and stand and placed them on the small trolley he pulled out from under the table. Then, he picked it back up and returned it to the cupboard. Hailey pictured him using it on the other girls, and it raised the hairs on her neck and the heat on her anger. She could feel the coldness of the gun in her back. All she needed was the opportune moment, but she still wanted him to talk to her. "Edward, how do the voices know who needs purification?" He faced her and frowned. *"They just know."* He moved slowly towards her. "Why did you do it?" she asked as she slowly reached for her gun. He smiled. *"It's time for you to find out. We must begin."* He was beside her in an instant and had his arm wrapped around her throat. He smothered her mouth with a cloth smelling of something sweet. Her hand fell from the gun and grabbed his arm, tugging. She thrashed around and tried to hit him with her elbow, but he kept dodging it so she made another reach for the gun but passed out even before her fingers grazed it. She went limp, then he laid her out on the table gently and began undressing her. He found the gun she had stashed and placed it on the trolley he had pulled up beside his thigh. He tossed a small cloth on top. Once her shirt was off, he laid out his scalpels and ran his fingers over them gently, loving the way the light made them glint.

*   *   *   *

Bobby and Gabe stood over the hole in the kitchen floor. They could see stairs leading down but nothing beyond. "I'll go first," Bobby whispered, looking over at Gabe. He nodded. They both pulled out their guns, and Bobby started down the steps. Gabe followed, and soon, they were both enveloped in darkness. Once they reached the bottom of the stairs, they heard Mozart flowing softly from somewhere. Gabe pulled out his penlight and quickly scanned the room. There was nothing around them except for a large metal door about four paces to their right. "It must be coming from there," Gabe whispered. Quietly, they advanced on the door. He waved at Gabe to wait on the side as he started to open the door.

*   *   *   *

He tied up her ankles and wrists and then selected a small scalpel with a long blade and held it up. The voices were mute; all he could hear was the steady breathing of his angel on the table and the soothing rhythm of Mozart. He brought the blade down towards her chest and began his first incision.

She started to moan and awoke with a scream in her throat. She tasted wet cloth and realized he had gagged her. Suddenly, she felt the burning pain on her chest, and she clenched her jaw. She closed her eyes tight to clear them of the fogginess the chloroform had caused and opened them again to watch as he lowered the scalpel and cut into her again. His eyes held a dark, vacant stare while her mind began running with escape plans. She had been trained for anything, but at this moment, she could think of nothing to help her. Just as he was about to make another incision, the door behind him swung open. She watched as Bobby crawled into the room and glanced around. He then stood up and began walking towards them gun raised.

*   *   *   *

He felt the air shift in the room just as he was about to make another cut. He slowly placed the scalpel down and straightened. "Who are you?" he asked without turning around. All he got for a response was the slow clicking of the hammer of a gun being pulled back. "How did you find my secret?" He turned slowly. "It doesn't matter really, because you won't be leaving."

*   *   *   *

Bobby didn't see him reach for the gun he had under the cloth on the trolley. Nor did he feel the punch of the bullet as it entered his chest and ripped a hole in his heart. Just as Edward didn't notice as Hailey used the scalpel he had left beside her to cut through her restraints and slip off the other side of the table. She held the scalpel in her right hand. Going low, she began a slow crab walk around the table. Just as she was about to attack, Gabe entered the room at a roll and fired two shots at Edward.

She stood there with his blood splattered over her face, and her chest bleeding from the incisions he had made while Gabe kneeled beside Bobby. "He's dead." She dragged her gaze over to Bobby's body. Studying the lifelessness of him, she picked up her shirt and held it over her wounds then went and crouched down on the other side of Bobby and rested her hand over his eyes, closing them. She looked over at Gabe. He still had his fingers on Bobby's wrist. She took his hand in hers. "Gabe. It's over. We stopped him." She released his hand and looked over to where Edward's body had fallen. There, in a pool of blood, his body was sprawled out. His eyes were open, but she knew he was dead from the two huge holes in his chest where Gabe had shot him. He didn't even have a chance to shoot back. Hailey hadn't known Gabe had it in him. She had a new respect for him. She went over to one of the cupboards and started searching for something to bandage herself up with when they both heard the crash above them then the running of feet. A minute later, the room was bursting with cops, and Hailey wanted nothing more than to hand this all over to them and head home. She let the medics tend to her chest while she answered some questions thrown at her from a cop who looked young enough to barely be out of high school, then she pushed up off the table and walked out the door.

Epilogue

Hailey sat at the table waiting for Gabe to show up. It had been a year since Bobby's funeral, and she had seen very little of Gabe. She tried to keep in contact with him, but it was hard when he wouldn't return her calls. The waiter brought her a salad and a new glass of water, and she had just settled in to eat when the chair across from her was pulled out. Waiting while he placed his order, she studied his face. He was rough shaven with dark circles under his blood-shot eyes. She kept getting whiffs of stale beer and guessed it was coming from him. The waiter left, and she smiled at him. "How have you been, Gabe?" Leaning back in his chair, he took a swallow of the beer the waiter had set in front of him. "Drunk." She watched as he scowled. "Stop blaming yourself for his death. You didn't kill him. Edward Mercurial pulled the trigger, not you, Gabe." He set his chair down. "I know that, Hailey. That's why I'm leaving the force and moving. I'm done, Hailey, just done." He looked so worn-out and defeated Hailey ached for him. "I hope it works for you, and if you ever need anything, call me." They finished their meals, said their good-byes, and left in opposite directions.

LaVergne, TN USA
13 October 2009
160758LV00009B/74/P